Molly

Molly

nancy j. jones

crown publishers   new york

Published by Crown Publishers, 201 East 50th Street, New York, New York 10022. Member of the Crown Publishing Group.

Random House, Inc. New York, Toronto, London, Sydney, Auckland
www.randomhouse.com

Crown is a trademark and the Crown colophon is a registered trademark of Random House, Inc.

Printed in the United States of America

Design by Barbara Sturman

Library of Congress Cataloging-in-Publication Data
Jones, Nancy J.
      Molly / by Nancy J. Jones.—1st ed.
      I. Title
   PS3560.05229M6   2000
   813'.54—dc21   99-39920
                                                          CIP

ISBN 0-609-60462-7

10 9 8 7 6 5 4 3 2 1

First Edition

This novel is dedicated,

in loving memory,

to my mother, Jean Quivey Jones.

Molly is inspired by the title character of Vladimir Nabokov's *Lolita*. I have the utmost respect for Nabokov—as both a writer and a scholar—and ultimately, I hope my vision of Molly Liddell pays tribute to him and his literary creation.

I have written my novel so that the reader unfamiliar with *Lolita* will be able to read *Molly* as a work complete in and of itself. However, the *Lolita* and Nabokov scholar will, I hope, take some delight in uncovering various literary and scholarly allusions in my novel.

"Help me, Peneus! Open the earth to enclose me, or change my form, which has brought me into this danger!"

Daphne to her father, the river god,
upon her pursuit by Apollo,
from *Bulfinch's Mythology*

Molly

FOREWORD

Girlhood friendships are like none other. Equal parts intrigue, discovery, and intoxication, they provide a refuge from which the friends explore and test the world beyond. Yet that safety is illusive, the sense of invincibility it fosters, false.

My best friend was Molly Liddell. By the time she was twelve, both her parents and her brother were dead. Five years later—and sometime after escaping from the stepfather who stole her childhood—she herself died in childbirth. She was not yet eighteen. Had she lived, she would have been sixty-five today.

How many times, when I learned of her death, I wondered if I could have saved her. How many times I felt sure that it was I, above all others, who had failed her. The secrets I kept from my mother, my reluctant participation in her escapades, my awe at her bravado. But I saw nothing ominous in Molly's flirtations and performances. Indeed, I lived for them. I did not know they foreshadowed her undoing. Nor could I know how Molly's fate would alter mine.

I am an old woman now. Yet after all these years, Molly still haunts me. When I close my eyes at night, she looms before me as I knew her in childhood—eyes flashing, strands of hair escaping from her auburn braids, tickling the nape of her neck, damp against her forehead. She stands in green rubber boots, her sleeveless undershirt slipping off one shoulder, arms outstretched, one bare, downy leg thrust forward, poised before a puddle in the dirt road that ran from the edge of town between towering rows of corn. She tips her head back and laughs, anticipating the squishy splash of brown, the suck and pull on her boots, the glorious splatter of mud against her legs. I want to catch her in my arms, feel again her skin warm and moist against mine.

Then the face before me changes. Her cheeks hollow and pale, and the perspiration at her temples now betrays her long and futile labor. Her mouth hangs open, her breathing shallow. Just before I fall asleep, her glazed eyes search the blank wall opposite her bed, then drop to the still and silent form she clutches to her breast.

But in the morning, as I watch through my window, Molly reappears, lithe and barefoot in the wet grass. She squares her shoulders and faces east, bathing herself in the liquid light streaming over the plains. *Arms winging skyward, fingers fluttering in the eddies of sunshine, she flings one leg into the air and launches herself into currents of gold and crimson that carry her aloft.*

I cannot bring her back, any more than I can reshape my own life. But I can reclaim her—and thus myself as well. Perhaps if I tell you what I knew of her from childhood and gleaned from the diaries and letters she left to me, you will see her as I do—as a fragrant promise, attainable but elusive as the wisps of hair escaping from her braids, as laughter dissolving in the wind.

ELIZABETH ANNE THURMONT

February 14, 2000

Charleston, Illinois

part one

how the lens of age transforms the vision. I am speaking not of the reading glasses to which I long ago surrendered, but of the quality of light that suffuses my days, lingering on each bronze expanse of wheat, the broad, blue reach of sky, illuminating the air itself till I am charged at once with contentment and expectation. The young are deluded in the belief that they alone possess life's essence, that all else around them is mere husk. I know, for I was young once, too.

Growing up in the 1940s, I felt only the blandness of things. Charleston was like so many other Midwestern towns. Elms and oaks shaded sleeping summer streets, disturbed only by the shriek of children, the shrill r-i-i-n-g, r-i-i-n-g of bicycle bells, the slap of jump ropes on sidewalks. Even downtown, despite the allure of the sweet-shop soda fountain and Will

7

Rogers Theater, held little enchantment. I loved to visit my father's law office on the east side of Sixth Street, to gaze at the shelves of gilt-edged books and pivot in my father's leather chair, but I grew bored by the succession of grocery stores and clothing shops and waited on one aching leg, then the other, while my mother selected a roast at the Piggly Wiggly, a Sunday hat with roses and netting at the Dress Well Shop next to Wolff's Drug Store.

The land itself seemed to ache for more. In summer, cicadas droned in the trees, as if the leaves themselves were chanting some green and humid prayer for release. Other days, roiling clouds blotted out the sun, the air sparked and cracked, and lightning shattered the sky into desperate fragments. Then the rain cascaded down, pelting wheat and corn and soy, relentless and insistent, drowning out everything but the doleful boom of thunder, rolling, tolling its despair.

In winter, when the sun rose late and low, snow blanketed the fields with silence, and the wind scoured the streets, whistling a discordant hymn that fueled my discontent.

But there was more. The pain of the Depression and the shadow of Hitler had stripped the town of life and men—which then, I thought, were one and the same—and I shrank from a future of sewing circles, church suppers, and the mending, ironing, and canning that filled the days of so many of the women I knew. Even their gossip was a thin and flavorless broth like that our mothers made in the lean years when we often went without meat. It did not nourish; indeed, it brought on a wasting disease that ate away the spirit as well as the flesh.

Molly Liddell felt the same as I. Together, we devoured every morsel from the outside world—magazines, newsreels, radio programs, films—savoring Elizabeth Taylor's triumph as National Velvet, Marlene Dietrich's victorious return from the front lines, Tom Mix's adventures in the Wild, Wild West. Our own lives, we knew, would unfold, petal by lustrous petal, somewhere far beyond the horizon.

How could I have known our youthful longing, so strong at times it singed our skin, would lead to Molly's ruin—and my own transformation?

In fifth grade, Molly and I began a ritual. Every day after school, we traced the same route, from the college to town square, then to the park, or, sometimes, for variety, the reverse. As we walked, we plotted our escape, to California or Paris or New York. With the money we coaxed from our parents in return for dusting knickknacks, we swilled down cherry Cokes and daydreams at the Corner Confectionery on the square. Mimicking the high-school kids who huddled in the turquoise vinyl booths and fed the jukebox, we jitterbugged across the red linoleum tiles to the big band sound of Tommy Dorsey, convinced that if we twirled fast enough, we might, like Dorothy, not be in Kansas anymore.

But I never dreamed that we might whirl apart. When we danced, we melted into a luminous being that outshone the sun.

The floor beneath us vibrated, and I could feel the molecules of oxygen and carbon dioxide careening and colliding as we set them into motion.

Afterward, panting at the counter, we spooned rivers of steaming chocolate and melting ice cream into our mouths. The boys in the booths eyed Molly and nudged one another. Even then, her high jinks charged the sugary air with static that set them off like Roman candles. She was slim and quick, and her short, flared skirt skimmed and skipped across her thighs as she swiveled on her stool.

Molly knew the boys were watching her. Crossing one leg high over the other, she bent toward me, her breath sticky with maraschino cherries and mischief. "What do you think about him?" she said. "Shall I ask him to dance?" She nodded so the boy in question would know she was talking about him. Then, still flushed from our last dance, she slipped down from her stool, sashayed over, and tapped him on the shoulder.

"Got a quarter?" she asked.

He must have been sixteen, lanky and blond, with an Adam's apple that bobbed up and down in reply. He extracted some change from his jeans pocket and guided her over to the juke-box. Molly stood on tiptoe, examining the song titles, all the while running one saddle-shoe-clad foot up and down her other leg. She punched a few numbers, and he led her to the dance floor.

I watched from my stool, tapping my feet on the rungs in time to the music. The boy reeled her in and out, putting her through somersaults and back flips, his hands now on the back of her legs, at her waist, beneath her arms, as he propelled her across the room and through the air. Once he boosted her up till she stood on his shoulders beneath the high tin ceiling. She arched her back, her unfurled fingers pointing toward the sky—a fantastic creature of vapor and light. Then, sensing the indrawn breath of her audience, Molly leapt forward, into the waiting air. The boy held out his hands and caught her. She extended her legs into a perfect split, hovering in his arms for one infinite moment before jumping to the floor.

I pushed away the rest of my sundae. Molly was my partner. I hardly knew as I watched whether I wanted to be in her place, so I could feel the rough hands of the boy against my back, at my waist, supporting my legs, or whether I wanted to be the boy himself, so I could be the one who lifted Molly to my shoulders and caught her in my arms. Perhaps I sensed then what it was that one day would take her away from me, that would separate us forever.

The music stopped. The boy brought Molly's hand to his lips. She curtseyed, skipped to my side, and hopped back up on her stool, where Mr. Palmer, the sweet shop's owner, clapped loud and long. With a deep bow, he presented her a box of his house chocolate–peanut butter fudge.

"Here," she said, rummaging beneath the lid with her sweaty fingers and handing me a slab. "We'll eat the rest tonight." She stuffed a whole piece in her mouth.

I nibbled on mine, let the salty sweet crumbs dissolve on my tongue like a promise. The boy was nothing to Molly. It was I she loved, I who would spend the night whispering beneath her pink gingham covers. My world had only trembled; now it was solid once again.

In the beginning, I couldn't believe Molly had chosen me as her best friend. It was not a gradual process. Rather, the first day of first grade, as we sat at our desks, unpacking our lunch pails, Molly reached across the aisle and tapped me on the arm.

I jumped and pulled back from her touch. I had watched her under cover of reading my primer that morning. Her braids were untamed, and her skirt was shorter than the other girls'. She wore a private, inward smile, but she turned the pages of her book as if every lift and flutter of her fingers were a public performance. Her stagy unconcern attracted and unsettled me.

"Trade you my apple for your peanut butter cookies," she said, flourishing her apple like a carnival prize.

It was an outrageous offer—what child would trade away her cookies for a piece of fruit? But Molly held herself with such assurance, chin jutting out in challenge and conquest, that I found myself handing over the special peanut butter cookies my mother had baked for my first lunch away from home before I considered a retort.

"You want to come to my house after school?" She talked with her mouth full of my cookies and licked her fingers with a deliberateness at once magnanimous and self-satisfied. "I've got a secret hiding place I'll show you."

"Okay," I said, "but I have to ask my mom." The day no longer seemed as terrifying as it had that morning when I sat down at my hard, wooden desk and stared at our young and solemn teacher, Miss Hamilton, handing out our workbooks. The heavy smell of chalk irritated my nose, I sneezed, and a phalanx of strange faces turned in unison to stare at me.

"Bless you," Miss Hamilton said.

I lowered my eyes, willing the heat to leave my face. "Excuse me," I said.

Now the shame and terror of the morning faded. I had a friend, and a fierce and dazzling one at that.

And so I went, elated that Molly had asked me and not one of the other girls, whose braids were glossier, hands daintier, smiles saucier. In the warm autumn dirt of her backyard, we scrambled on hands and knees beneath a curtain of forsythia.

"Wait till you see," Molly said, sitting cross-legged in the dark green light. She dug in the soft dirt with a small, sharp rock till she uncovered a green metal box. Brushing off the dirt, she lifted the box and held it out to me.

I took it, uncertain.

"Open it," she said.

I did. I don't know what I expected—stolen treasure, a pirate's ear, a shrunken head—but the box contained only three smooth gray stones. I raised my eyebrows and looked at her.

"Take them out," she said, leaning forward. "Look at them closely."

On the surface of the stones were the impressions of tiny three-lobed creatures that resembled scorpions.

"Trilobites," Molly said. "They're five hundred million years old. My dad gave them to me. He's a scientist."

"Why don't you keep them in your room?" I ran my fingers over the surface of the stones. I had never held anything so ancient.

"Mum," she said, as if that were sufficient explanation. Then, when I continued to stare at her: "She doesn't like Daddy's science stuff in the house. She says it makes her feel like she's living with dead things."

"But they're only stones," I said.

"Maybe you can come to Daddy's lab with me." Molly grabbed my hand. "He has a whole wall of jars filled with pickled frogs and brains and even a real skeleton. His name's Dem Bones."

"My dad's a lawyer," I said. "We can go to his office sometime, too. He has rows of books that go clear to the ceiling and a ladder that you climb to reach the ones on the top shelves. It has wheels."

"What about your mum?" Molly asked. "Do you think she'd bake us more cookies? My mum only makes hors d'oeuvres." She wrinkled her nose.

"Sure," I said, "she'll even let us help. And you can lick the beaters." I had something Molly wanted after all, so I pressed my advantage. "She has a darkroom, too, and we can help her develop photographs."

From that day on, we were inseparable. Even rainy days, closeted in her room or mine, were magical. The rain streamed down the window panes, making the world outside wavy and blurred. The oak and elm trees ran like watercolors into the soggy earth, and the gingerbread on the Victorian houses across the street melted like brown sugar, dissolving in the watery air.

Warm and dry, Molly and I sat side by side on the bed, shoes kicked off, backs against the cool plaster wall. Often we drew. Beneath a drawing of a winged horse, Molly printed in awkward block letters, "Have you ever seen a horse fly?" On another picture of a two-by-four with a smiling face, stick arms and legs, I wrote, "Or a board walk?" And finally, below a drawing of a brown cow with wet, dark eyes and huge, pink tongue, "What about a cow lick?"

At Thanksgiving, we made greeting cards with our company name, Hand Maid, on the reverse. We gave these to each other. I still have the one Molly gave me, green construction paper cut in the shape of a fir tree, that says, "I'm pining for you this Christmas!" She had glued real pine needles on the tree.

We were drawing in my room, sprawled out on the braided rug, when my mother came to the door. "Girls, Molly will have to spend the night. Michael has pneumonia, Molly. Your parents have rushed him to the hospital." She knelt on the rug and put her arms around Molly. "Don't worry, sweetheart, he'll be okay."

But Michael, Molly's younger brother, would not be okay. Indeed, nothing would be quite the same again.

~~~

That day was Saturday. The next morning, we awoke to a howling wind. Snow was falling fast and hard, the world was white and veiled. Molly's parents were still at the hospital with Michael. Charleston was paralyzed. Molly would not be able to join her family, nor would we be able to attend church.

"Mrs. Thurmont," Molly said, "we have to have a service." Her gray-green eyes were eager, desperate.

An hour later, we sat rigid and attentive in the high-backed chairs of the dining room, where Molly and I had set up a sanctuary. She distributed a homemade bulletin of the worship service. Now we rose from our chairs while my mother led us in the opening hymn. I lit the candles on the "altar"—my mother's sideboard.

Molly herself stood at the head of the table, solemn in her ministerial robes—one of my father's white shirts, buttoned up the back, and a red satin bow tied around her neck. This was the same uniform she wore in the choir, for she loved singing, and it was the choir that enticed her to Sunday services without so much as a cross word to her mother.

Folding her hands in front of her, Molly nodded to me, and I recited Psalm 23, which we both knew by heart. Near the end, she joined in: "Surely goodness and mercy shall follow me all the days of my life; and I shall dwell in the house of the Lord for ever."

Molly bowed her head. "Let us pray," she said and led us in the Lord's Prayer.

Mother started us off on "Soldiers of the Cross," and while we sang, my father passed the collection plate, into which we all contributed pennies and nickels for the mission.

For her sermon, Molly selected a personal theme. Weekdays, Mrs. Liddell regularly scolded Molly for dawdling over breakfast, and Molly responded by moving still more slowly. In consequence, she often arrived at school in the middle of the Pledge of Allegiance. By Thanksgiving, the principal had warned Mrs. Liddell that she could not tolerate Molly's tardiness anymore. One more occurrence, and Molly would be sent home. Thus it was that Molly titled her sermon "Are You Ever Late?" She preached on the dangers of living by the clock, urged us, her congregation, to "enjoy every bite of French toast, every bit of maple syrup" as if it were our last.

For the final hymn, Molly had chosen "All Things Bright and Beautiful," and as we sang, holding hands, I thought no one was as brave and bright and beautiful as she.

the next day, Michael remained in the hospital, and Mrs. Liddell did not leave his side. After school, Dr. Liddell invited us to his laboratory.

Molly's father was a biology professor at the college. He was an enigma in Charleston, revered for his modest intelligence and scientific dedication, but suspect for his preference for solitude—his long hours in the lab, his late-night walks through the silent streets.

Although he was in his mid-fifties, much older than his wife, he was devoted to her. He called her "my love," "my clever Kitty." Yet he was more at ease among his jars of frogs and fetal pigs. When he and Catherine took us on picnics to Lincoln's nearby family farm, he always disappeared with his butterfly net.

"Kitty," he would say later, thrusting the net out in front of him, "look, dear. Look, girls. Isn't she a beauty? Molly, do you know what kind of butterfly she is?" And he would drop to his knees, eager as a boy.

Mrs. Liddell would sigh and lean back on her blanket while we helped him identify his specimen.

I loved to visit his laboratory.

That Monday afternoon, he showed us how to scrape skin cells from the inside of our cheeks to study under a microscope. We opened our mouths wide, held our breath, while he took a clean scalpel and gently scraped away a filmy substance, which he smeared on a slide. The cold metal tickled, and we pinched each other's forearms so we wouldn't laugh.

"Cheek cells are called squamous epithelial cells, girls," he said and nodded to the microscope under which he had placed the slides.

I put my eye to the scope and held my breath so it wouldn't blur. The cells danced beneath my eyes like a kaleidoscope.

Afterward, Dr. Liddell let us study Dem Bones, pointing out clavicle and scapula, tibia and fibula.

"Do you remember this one, Molly?" He pointed to the upper arm bone.

"Humerus," she shouted.

"How about you, Betsy? What's this one?" Dr. Liddell gestured to the upper leg.

But I was too shy to answer.

"Femur," Molly said, nudging me.

When our lesson was over, we wheeled the skeleton down the aisle to his outpost in the back of the lab. Molly began to dance with Dem, causing his arms and legs to flail back and forth, grazing the desks.

Dr. Liddell said only, "Molly, remember how old Mr. Bones is. Take care of him."

And she did, walking him respectfully to his place, then wrapping her arms around her father's waist and tilting her face to his.

"Oh, Daddy," she said, "I'd never hurt Mr. Bones."

He ran his hand through her hair. "Of course you wouldn't, Molly," he said. "Sometimes we don't realize how we hurt the ones we love." Then he looked out the window, stroking her hair and pressing her to him.

two days later, Michael died. Mrs. Liddell was incapacitated.

She hired a housekeeper to cook and clean and care for Molly. Miss Frazier was cranky and constipated and hung her enema bag from the bathroom showerhead. She stocked up on prunes and made prune cake for Molly's sixth birthday on Valentine's Day. I was invited to Molly's party, and we sat in the living room, just the two of us and Molly's parents, choking down the dreary cake beneath a large oil painting of Michael in his christening gown which hung above the fireplace mantel. No matter where you sat in the room, he stared at you with sad, flat eyes.

"Saint Michael," Molly whispered to me.

Still, by summer Mrs. Liddell had recovered sufficiently from Michael's death to take over the household chores again, and she began to invite me to spend afternoons at their house. She and Dr. Liddell had honeymooned in Barcelona. I loved the brightly painted pottery and miniature oils of matadors and bulls scattered about the house in gaudy, dusty abandon. And when Mrs. Liddell put on her flamenco music, Molly and I were on our feet, grabbing the castanets she held out, ready to dance around the room.

Often, she took us to the movies.

I loved these outings, suffused with glamour and daring. Mrs. Liddell had the allure and presence of a starlet. Mr. Parker, who owned the movie house, always escorted us to our seats himself, taking Mrs. Liddell's coat and handing her in with a deep bow.

One evening when Dr. Liddell was working late, she took us to see *How Green Was My Valley*. Afterward, Mr. Parker saw us home. It was a humid night, and Mrs. Liddell carried her sweater in the crook of her arm. She wore a navy-and-white polka-dotted halter dress that swept down over her breasts and gathered beneath them at the fitted waist. Her skin was misty and pink from the heat and gave off a faint scent of jasmine. She shooed Molly and me ahead of her, her arm tucked through his elbow.

When we reached Molly's house, Mr. Parker ushered us up the front walk.

"Why, I declare," Mrs. Liddell said, "you are every bit the gentleman. I am entirely in your debt. Dr. Liddell, you know, is often kept away at the laboratory. We are so grateful to be seen safely home, aren't we, girls?"

Molly and I were still spellbound by the movie and intent on becoming Welsh miners. The prospect of life underground, our faces blackened with coal dust, held far more appeal than a walk down Charleston's staid streets with portly Mr. Parker, who cleared his throat far more often than necessary. However, I couldn't fail to be impressed with the way Mrs. Liddell's polka dots danced about her legs as she turned to say good night.

Long afterward, as I lay in my own bed, I smelled the cloud of jasmine that emanated from Mrs. Liddell and rippled through the heavy air on the swish and swirl of her skirt.

A from that night on, Mr. Parker always walked us home from the movies. And despite the hint of scandal that clung to Mrs. Liddell like cashmere, I wished my mother were more like her, more extravagant and exciting. The women in my family, too, were the stuff of legend, but legend of a very different kind.

My great-grandmother McCracken's husband was decapitated in a tornado that devastated their corn harvest. That fall, however, Esther McCracken bought a new team of mules and planted two hundred acres in winter wheat. In long brown skirts and high, laced boots, she worked the fields herself the following summer. Great-grandma McCracken not only drove the plow and raked the hay, she also amassed a fortune in grain futures— which educated her three daughters and put my mother through the University of Chicago, where she received a degree in photography. Much later still, her money put me through Harvard Law School.

The McCracken women were strong and stout. I inherited their sturdy bones and large hands—and their tendency to put on weight. Hearty fare, especially home-baked goods, was their only vice, and they'd won their share of prizes at the Coles County Fair. They also were highly regarded—in the Grange, the Women's Club, the First Baptist Church, Charleston Community Bank. They managed to combine a zeal for women's suffrage with a passionate commitment to church and community that caused town leaders to overlook their eccentricities. Great-grandma had marched on the picket line with strikers for the International Ladies Garment Workers Union in 1910. She had embroidered a quotation from Elizabeth Cady Stanton that hung over her desk:

> The talk of sheltering woman from the fierce storms of life is the sheerest mockery, for they beat on her from every point of the compass, just as they do on man, and with more fatal results, for he has been trained to protect himself, to resist, and to conquer.

Even after Edith McCracken Keckler, my mother's mother, lost a son to suicide and sold the farm, she found a job teaching French at Teachers College High, where she later became principal. (She'd spent a summer at the Sorbonne in Paris before she married my grandfather.)

My mother inherited not only the McCracken money but also the McCracken spirit. She had suffered three miscarriages before I was born, but I knew nothing of these until after her death. I think it was my mother's own misfortune, as well as her sense of sisterhood, that led to her ambivalence about Catherine Liddell. She refused to shun her when other women in the community began to drop Mrs. Liddell from their guest lists.

Yet that fall, after Molly and I started second grade, my mother said once, "What good do Hollywood looks do a woman when she can't even control her own daughter?"

We were in the darkroom, and my mother was extracting a photograph from a tray. Molly had been sent home from school that morning for wearing lipstick.

"Don't forget, Elizabeth," my mother said, immersing the print in a second bath, "vanity has been the downfall of many a woman."

But I did not believe her. I wished more than ever I were as bold and beautiful as Molly.

$\mathscr{A}$ soon, however, the whole country had the chance to show its bravery. After the Japanese bombed Pearl Harbor, our lives changed. Young men left Charleston in numbers, signing up to fight the enemy in Europe and the Pacific.

I helped my mother roll bandages for the Red Cross—proud of the gold-striped thousand-hour service ribbon she earned and wore on the breast of her service uniform. My mother rolled bandages faster than a cat could unroll a ball of yarn.

Mrs. Liddell flaunted her patriotism like a fine mink coat. She prided herself on her ability to stretch her "points" at the grocery store, and she was one of the first to donate her stockings to the war effort.

Molly and I loved to watch her put on leg makeup—she had glamorous legs, a dancer's legs, though she did no calf raises, stretches, or exercises whatsoever—and we often lay on the floor, legs in the air, beside her, while she waited for the makeup to dry.

"Never, never leave the house without putting your best foot forward, girls," she said, turning her head to us sagely, her curls spilling across the braided rug like tongues of flame.

Neither Molly's father nor mine enlisted in the war. Dr. Liddell was too old and his work too necessary to the college, and my father had poor eyesight. Still, they were active on the home front.

I was thrilled when my father exchanged his dark suit and tie for overalls to captain the Victory Garden Committee. He even plowed the garden himself, with a Belgian draft horse named Buddy he'd borrowed from a farmer, stopping at the end of each row to catch his breath and mop his forehead. Sometimes he let me hold the traces and cluck to Buddy.

Dr. Liddell joined the Civilian Defense Corps to watch for enemy planes from a tower that rose above the trees at the edge of town.

In the summer of 1942, after school was out, he took Molly and me with him to the lookout. He had the four to six A.M. shift and woke us in the cold dark with mugs of hot cocoa. After nightfall, Charleston was under blackout—people tacked blankets to their windows and the streetlights stayed dark—and Dr. Liddell drove the two miles to the tower with the black Packard's headlights off, creeping along at less than ten miles per hour as he peered into the dark. Molly and I sat in the backseat, clutching the binoculars, flashlight, and the plastic wheel bearing the silhouettes of the enemy planes—Japanese bombers like the ones that struck Pearl Harbor, German fighters like those that had shot down American pilots in Europe. The cool wind fluttered around the car in warning, and we felt part of something larger than ourselves, imagining men in towns across the country crawling through the black streets to take up their nighttime posts.

By the time we reached the tower, we'd grown accustomed to the darkness. The wind swirled about our legs as we climbed the wooden stairs. Molly scampered up the steps two at a time, while I followed at a prudent pace, clinging to the metal railing that bit at my hands. Once we reached the platform, we settled down on a blanket, our backs against the railing, peering at the sky till our eyes stung.

There were no planes, but stars spattered the sky. The Milky Way cut a phosphorescent path across the heavens.

"There, girls, the Big Dipper at five o'clock," Dr. Liddell said, pointing out the constellations.

While we wished on shooting stars, he told us about meteors that hurtled through space at such unimaginable speed and with such ferocious intensity that they burned up on entering the Earth's atmosphere. We sat on either side of him, leaning into the rough wool of his overcoat, our legs covered by a second blanket, scratchy against our skin.

As the night wore on, he told us about the war, about the chaplain of the U.S.S. *New Orleans* who advised the gunners that fateful Sunday in Pearl Harbor to "praise the Lord and pass the ammunition." About GIs in the Pacific who went for weeks without a hot meal, battling not only the enemy but also sweltering heat, swarms of insects, malaria that raged in the body like the fires of hell, and rot that ate away at their toenails and feet. About women who tied their hair back in bandannas, pulled on jeans and workshirts, heavy suede gloves, and goggles to wield acetylene torches in factories that built the weapons and warships to help the U.S. military beat back the Germans and the Japanese.

When we began to shiver, he uncapped his silver thermos and poured us cups of steaming coffee with milk and sugar. We tipped our heads back and let the warm, sweetly acid liquid glide down our throats. My mother had sent along a blue-and-white cloth napkin wrapped around her famous mile-high biscuits, and we stuffed ourselves with those as well, all the while keeping our eyes on the sky. We pinched each other to stay awake—we would not let our country down.

After a time, we sat in silence, waiting for the black to fade to blue, then pink and orange. Just before the sun burst over the horizon, the birds began to sing in the trees below us, first cardinals, then wrens, warbling their morning hymns, oblivious to the danger we had once again been spared.

At the end of our shift, we bowed our heads in a prayer of thanks and praise. God was on our side; he would continue to protect us.

We were hungry. But Dr. Liddell stayed on to chat with Mr. Cook, who took the six-to-eight watch. Molly and I began to kick our legs back and forth through the empty air as we sat resting our arms on the railing. Our stomachs rumbled like stampeding cattle. Dr. Liddell, however, noticed nothing, and remained deep in conversation about the forecast for spring wheat.

Still, we joined Dr. Liddell on his shift every week from that day until school began in September. Even the prospect of a delayed breakfast never kept us from accepting his invitations. We loved the early-morning vigils, prayed we might be the first to spot the flash of wings far overhead, pictured President and Mrs. Roosevelt awarding us medals at the White House. But no enemy planes appeared.

Nonetheless, we had our moment of fame, flanking Dr. Liddell in a photograph for the local paper. PROFESSOR LEADS VICTORY EFFORTS, the headline read. Our own names appeared in the caption: "Molly Liddell and Elizabeth Thurmont assist Molly's father, Dr. Howard Liddell, in keeping the skies safe for Charleston." I taped the clipping in my scrapbook, where I kept a lock of my baby hair and an article on Great-grandma McCracken's arrest for collaring a drunk in a speakeasy raid.

dr. liddell died of a heart attack on Monday, October 2, 1944. Molly cried all night in my mother's arms. She would not eat or sleep.

At the funeral, Catherine wore a black wool suit and black veiled hat. She dabbed at her eyes with a white lace handkerchief, and her voice trembled as she sang the final hymn, "A Mighty Fortress Is Our God." Molly stood impassively, a few feet from her mother's side, mouthing the words. Afterward, Mrs. Liddell stumbled as she left the sanctuary, clutching at the wooden backrest of the adjacent pew. My father leapt from his seat and grabbed her by the elbow, leading her, weeping, up the aisle. Molly trailed behind, her eyes on her black-patent Molly Janes, the ones she had begged her mother for months to buy and which now slapped dully against the burgundy carpet.

Three weeks later, Mrs. Liddell invited us into her bedroom while she got ready to take us to the movies. As she leaned closer to the mirror to apply her lipstick, I noticed the wedding photograph of her and her husband had disappeared from the bureau.

mrs. liddell's moods, never predictable, grew more erratic and alarming. Once, Molly and I were in Mrs. Liddell's bedroom, Molly ironing the clean clothes while I folded them and hung them on hangers. I loved to help with the laundry at Molly's house. Mrs. Liddell wore lacy bras and panties, tailored slacks in taupe and wine, frothy playsuits with peek-a-boo cutouts—a vivid contrast to my mother's somber skirts, blouses, and sensible bloomers.

Molly was ironing her mother's polka-dotted halter dress, the same one she'd worn when Mr. Parker first began seeing us home from the movies.

"I wonder when we'll get breasts," Molly said now, running the iron over the dress's swollen folds.

My mother and I never talked about breasts. I imagined Molly and Mrs. Liddell, Molly flopped on her stomach, chin resting on her hands, at the end of her mother's bed, watching as Mrs. Liddell reached behind her back to close the hooks and eyes of her bra, while she explained about breasts. Catherine Liddell had beautiful breasts. In her halter dress, they seemed like oranges wrapped in tissue paper waiting to be plucked.

"My mother says breasts make you lose your balance," I said, making something up as I folded a stack of Dr. Liddell's handkerchiefs. "She says it makes it harder to ride a bike."

I had watched a woman with awkward, pendulous breasts trying to balance on a bicycle in the church parking lot that spring. She was small-boned and slender, but her breasts swayed before her like the pastry bags my mother filled with icing to decorate cakes. The woman's husband ran behind her, holding the back of her seat, but when he let go, she teetered sideways and lost her balance, dragged downward by her heavy breasts.

"My mum," said Molly, who was always the authority in such matters, "says nice breasts are two of the best assets a woman can have. She says, being as they're right there, out in front, breasts are the first things a man sees when he meets a woman. If they're droopy, he thinks you're dull. If they're like pancakes, then he thinks you're mannish. But if they sit right up and say hello, then he naturally assumes you're a pleasant conversation-alist, someone who knows how to listen to a man and when to remark on what he says."

"I don't care," I said. "I don't want them. I want to play basketball. Breasts would be in the way."

I was at a loss when Molly talked this way, so I became stubborn, clinging to the opposite point of view no matter what I thought or felt. My own mother was so different from hers. We talked of books and politics and the economy in my home.

"You only say that because you probably won't get them anyway. My mum says your mum doesn't have breasts at all—just fat. So if you're skinny, you won't get them, and if you're fat, well, you'll just be fat." Molly stuck her tongue out at me.

"Yeah, well, I can run faster than you. Try to catch me."

I dropped the handkerchiefs and ran out of the door and down the hall to Molly's bedroom. She ran after me, but I slammed the door. When she began pounding on it, Mrs. Liddell called from the living room, "Girls, you're not a herd of elephants. If you don't behave, I'll send Betsy home."

She started up the stairs.

"Open the door," Molly said, "or I'll send you home."

I opened it as Mrs. Liddell reached the landing. It was then that we smelled the smoke.

Mrs. Liddell flew into her bedroom and emerged seconds later holding the dress. One of the breasts had been scorched. The fabric was black and gave off a chemical smell. I felt my face grow hot. It was my fault. I had taunted Molly. But Mrs. Liddell had forgotten me. She held the dress out in front of her.

"Mary Alice Liddell, how could you?" she said. Tears ran down her cheeks, and red welts rose on her slender neck.

"You're jealous of me. That's it, isn't it? You can't stand to have a mother who looks like a movie star. You miserable brat, you ought to be proud!"

With each word she took a step toward her daughter, and with each word Molly retreated backward down the hall till she reached her own room.

"What do you have to say for yourself?" Mrs. Liddell asked.

"I didn't mean it, Mummy," Molly said, shrinking back against the wall. "Really, I didn't mean it."

"Well, mean it or not, you ruined my favorite dress." Mrs. Liddell pursued Molly into her room. I hung back in the hall, keeping an eye on the stairs, but I could see and hear everything.

Mrs. Liddell threw the dress at Molly. "How would you like it if I ruined something of yours?" she asked, shaking Molly by the shoulders. "Well? Answer me."

"I wouldn't," Molly whispered.

Mrs. Liddell opened her daughter's closet and yanked Molly's blue-and-white sailor outfit off its hanger. "Here," she said, "this will teach you to take better care of your mother's things." She grabbed the scissors on Molly's desk. We had been cutting out costumes for our paper dolls from movie and fashion magazines earlier.

"No, Mummy, please, no." Now Molly was crying, too.

"This will teach you a lesson," her mother said. She held one corner of the sailor collar in her teeth, the other in her left hand, and began to cut through the fabric.

"Please, Mummy, please, don't do it. I promise I'll be good. You can take away my allowance, anything, only please don't ruin my sailor suit."

But Mrs. Liddell sliced the collar in half and cut deep slashes down the front of the entire blouse. She had stopped crying, but the welts on her neck deepened to a violent purple. She dropped the sailor costume to the floor and pulled a gingham romper out of the closet and snipped off the legs. Then she yanked Molly's green taffeta Christmas dress off its hanger and sliced away the puffy sleeves and the big satin bow at the back of the waist.

Molly ran at her mother and tried to wrestle the scissors from her hands. I was afraid Mrs. Liddell would stab her daughter. I had read of such things in the newspaper and wondered whether I could sneak to the phone and call the police.

"Get away from me!" Mrs. Liddell yelled. "Get away from me!" She held the scissors high above her head.

"I hate you!" Molly shrieked. "I hate you!"

"I hate you, too!" her mother wailed. "You've ruined my dress. What did I do to deserve a daughter like you? You're not to leave your room for the rest of the afternoon. Think about what you've done." She swept out of the room and slammed the door.

I went to Molly. She sat on the floor, the ruined dresses in her lap. It was one of the few times I saw her cry. "I'll kill her," she said, burying her head in her hands. "I'll kill her."

Downstairs, it was quiet. I stroked Molly's hair and stared at the posters of Alan Ladd and Veronica Lake on the wall. I had heard the talk at school about Mrs. Liddell. About why Mr. Parker gave Molly movie posters and no one else.

For the first time since we'd become friends, I realized how painful Molly's life was.

$\mathcal{A}$ a few months after her husband died, Catherine Liddell began throwing "Welcome Home" parties for wounded servicemen who'd been sent back from the front. At the same time, I began lying to my mother about what Molly and I did when I spent the night at her house. Saturday mornings, Catherine's reliable Packard would pull up in front of my house, and I'd run out with my overnight bag and a sack of cookies my mother had baked. The three of us nibbled on the cookies on the way to the grocery store, where Mrs. Liddell sent us on a mission for carrots, celery, cucumbers, olives—whatever we could manage within her allotted budget. We tallied up ration points, debated the merits of mustard and mayonnaise. Mrs. Liddell carried with her recipes she had torn from women's magazines, which she consulted as we gathered up our purchases.

In the afternoon, she armed us with feather dusters and sent us out into the living and dining rooms to rout whatever dust we found there while she prepared deviled eggs, pigs-in-a-blanket, trays of crudités. We dreaded her "inspections."

"Molly, you've left one of your socks beneath the davenport," she'd say.

Or "Girls, you've forgotten the ashtrays. I told you to put out ashtrays."

Or "Look at the lint on that rug. Did you run the sweeper, or simply admire it? These are veterans we are entertaining tonight. Men who fought for our freedom. Is this the best you can do for them?"

She flew around the rooms, straightening a lace doily here, a cushion there, putting candles on the dining room table, silk flowers on the coffee table. While Molly and I polished the silver, she set the table with fragile plates rimmed with roses.

She put recordings of *La Bohème* or *Madame Butterfly* on the phonograph and sang as she worked. Molly rolled her eyes at me and grinned. The silver polish lodged beneath our fingernails and gave them a metallic smell, but we shrugged off the drudgery and Mrs. Liddell's admonitions—we could scarcely wait for seven o'clock.

Catherine was too nervous to cook dinner, and too concerned about her figure to eat. Molly and I finished off the cookies my mother had sent along, helped ourselves to glasses of milk, brushed our teeth, scrubbed our faces, and pulled on our best Sunday dresses.

Then we joined Mrs. Liddell in her bedroom.

Seated at her vanity, she applied her lipstick, puckering her mouth before the mirror. "Always open your mouth when you apply your mascara—it makes your hand steadier," she advised as we watched, holding our breath.

She instructed us in all the rituals of womanhood—how to paint our nails candy-apple red, blowing on our fingers till the lacquer dried, how to hold a cigarette for a man to light.

We reveled in these moments in the intimacy of her room, inhaling the scent of polish and powder, spellbound by pots of azure and smoke. Stretched out across the chenille bedspread that tickled our thighs, Molly and I touched the rustling cascade of pearls Mrs. Liddell held out to us.

"A woman can never have too many pearls," she said. "Your father bought me these on our honeymoon in Spain. He said he'd dive for pearls himself, but I wouldn't hear of it."

She would hold the strand to her heart, gaze at the ceiling. I think sometimes she forgot we were there. Then Molly would crunch an apple and the spell would be broken.

"Mary Alice Liddell, haven't I told you not to eat in my bedroom? Now, shoo, both of you." She waved us out and closed the door.

We waited on the landing till she emerged, like an actress leaving her dressing room. Often, she wore a silk camellia in her hair, which fell in waves to her shoulders.

Mrs. Liddell glowed during her "soirées," as if she were lit from inside, like a lampshade. Once, at a dance at the Grange hall, she was mistaken for Rita Hayworth, and she had several of Hayworth's publicity photos, which she brought out to show her guests.

"What do you think?" she'd say, holding them out to a soldier no more than twenty-two or -three and tipping back her head. "Do you think I could be Rita's sister?"

"By golly, ma'am," he'd say, slapping his knee, "you make Rita look downright plain. They should have sent you over to entertain the troops. Now, that would have boosted our spirits."

"You're too kind," she'd say, resting her fingers on his shoulder, "but please, don't stand on ceremony. Call me Catherine, not ma'am. I'm not your mother, after all."

She allowed Molly and me to serve trays of canapés and glasses of champagne. The men joked with us, called us, "Hey, kiddo" and "sister," regaled us with tales of black nights bent low in foxholes, the sky exploding in fireworks, the rain of arms and legs and helmets that poured down in the aftermath of bombs and grenades. They told us of dogfights far above land and sea, of Flying Fortresses in tight formation, all eyes riveted on the horizon, scanning the sky for the dark specks that were German Luftwaffe fighters.

Often they wore their uniforms, let us touch the badges they'd earned. A dark, block-letter **A** on a field of green for the First Army that fought in Normandy, recaptured Paris, and was the first to cross the Rhine. The Seventh Army—a navy blue triangle emblazoned with the red-and-gold emblem of the division that swept into Sicily and southern France, up the Rhône, and into Munich. And Molly's favorite, the 101st Airborne "Screaming Eagle," an eagle's head on a black crest, with the letters AIRBORNE striding across a banner above the crest. The

Screaming Eagles screeched across the skies at Normandy and Bastogne, and we sat at the feet of Lt. Bill Johnson, the sad-eyed pilot with the crippled left leg who wore the Eagles' badge over his heart. He'd had to parachute from his burning plane and shattered his femur (we knew from studying Dem Bones how thick the femur was, winced at the impact it would take to pulverize that strong, defiant bone) so badly the doctors were unable to mend the break. Lieutenant Johnson walked with a mahogany cane topped with a silver eagle's head and—though he laughed and drank with the others—always seemed to be listening to some music deep inside. The drone of the engines? we wondered. The whine of wings as the damaged plane nosed forward and plunged toward the earth? Sometimes, after he'd had two or three drinks, he'd fall at Mrs. Liddell's feet, put his head on her knees, and weep while she stroked his hair.

After she sent us upstairs, we lay in the dark, listening to the men clinking their glasses, toasting her.

"You're what we've been fighting for," they said.

And "Lady, you're one fine dame."

In the mornings, Mrs. Liddell woke late and descended, crusty-eyed and blotchy-faced, to the kitchen, where Molly and I had mixed up pancakes and heated water for coffee. Sometimes she was too ill to go to church, and Molly and I went without her. I listened closely to the sermon and got a copy of the church bulletin so that I could tell my mother about the service. When we bowed our heads in prayer, I thanked God the Liddells attended a different church than mine. My mother would have grilled me on Mrs. Liddell's absence.

molly became more reckless after her father died. She flaunted a crimson scar on her knee, a wound from a fight at the ice-skating rink. To me, the scar made her leg even more beautiful, for it bloomed against her skin like an orchid.

Neither Molly nor I was allowed to go to the rink—no respectable children were. The crowd was rough.

That did not dissuade Molly. At recess on a clear, crisp day in the spring of our fifth-grade year, she slipped me a note: "Meet me on the basketball court after school. Mummy is taking Spanish lessons this afternoon, and she gave me money to take you to the movies. Let's go skating instead. Mum will be mooning over Señor Ortiz's accent all night, and she won't even think to ask us what was playing. Is it a date, mate?"

Later, bouncing a basketball up and down beneath the net, I tried to protest. "What if we get caught?" I asked. My mother was spending a few days in Chicago arranging for a show of her photographs, but she was sure to ask for a full report of my activities when she returned.

"We won't," said Molly. She blew a large pink bubble that burst and clung to her nose and mouth. "Come on," she said, scraping the gum off her face and popping it back in her mouth.

She linked her arm through mine, and I let her lead me down the street. The rink squatted on a barren plot of ground near the railroad tracks.

When we went inside, a woman with heavy breasts plastered against her belly took our money and directed us to a wall with shelves of skates arranged by size. Molly found a red pair, scuffed and faded, that matched her short red-and-white dress, while I settled on a pair that had once been white but now were yellow-gray. They smelled of sour milk, but I gritted my teeth and tugged them on. Molly was ready, and I was terrified of being left behind to make my way onto the ice alone.

I begged her to stand at the gate for a few minutes. Most of the skaters were older—fifteen or sixteen—and attended Charleston High. (Children from the "better" families in town, like Molly's and mine, attended Teachers College High.) Music of the sort you'd hear at a carnival blared from the loudspeaker, and to this, the skaters glided around the rink, a few in pairs, some alone, and most in awkward groups of five or six that jostled one another in mock indignation.

"Come on," Molly said, grabbing my hand and sailing out onto the ice.

I was tall, awkward for my age, and stumbled and fell right away. But Molly yanked me back up and dragged me behind her, till we were not only keeping pace with the other skaters but passing them. I locked my knees and allowed myself to be towed along, eyes closed, feeling her fingers at my wrist, the ice-blue air against my face.

"I'm going to let go now," Molly shouted and shoved me forward.

I careened into a knot of older boys huddled at the edge of the rink. One of them smirked and pulled me up by my arm, inspecting me.

"What's the matter, sister?" he said. "You need a man to take you around. I could show you a few other tricks while I'm at it."

"No . . . no, thank you. I'm so-sorry," I said. "Let me go, please."

The boy who gripped my arm smelled of beer and tobacco. He ran his free hand through his oiled hair and pushed up the sleeve of his T-shirt to admire his biceps.

Just then Molly skated to a halt in front of us. "What's going on?" she asked, sticking out her chin. "Why don't you let go of her and pick on someone your own size?"

The boy clenched my arm tighter, digging his fingers into my flesh. A savage purple bloom spread across my skin.

"You got no business here," he said.

He pulled me closer and wrapped his other arm around me. I felt something hard against the small of my back, in the vicinity of his fly.

He smirked again, as if he sensed my confusion, and said to Molly, "Go on. Scram. This is between her and me."

He thrust his pelvis forward to emphasize "me," so that I fluttered like a rag doll before him. My skates skidded out from under me, but he hoisted me up till my buttocks balanced on the bulge in his jeans.

Molly glanced from me to the boy and back again.

"No, it's not," she said, moving toward us, hands on her hips. "Her business is my business, and if I were you, I'd let go of her now. I'll call the manager and get you thrown out of here faster than you can tie your shoes. That is, if you know how to tie your shoes."

"Get out of here." The boy spat the words and shoved me toward Molly. "Both of you. And stay clear, sister, or you'll regret it."

I fell into her arms. She had never seemed more solid.

"You can't boss me. I'll go where I please," Molly shot back, her arms around me, but already he had turned his back on us, pulled a comb out of his back pocket, and begun slicking back his hair. She took me by the arm and led me to the gate.

"Watch this," she said after I stumbled to the bleachers. Then she was off, skating like a fury, spinning, pirouetting with such skill and venom that I knew she had been to the rink before. She darted among the skaters like a minnow, silver and slippery, and I longed to be the air in which she swam, to part before her and pour across her face.

The group of boys I had collided with had swaggered back onto the ice, elbowing and punching one another, their catcalls and shouts rising above the music. Molly flung her arms into her skating, gaining momentum, cutting in front of them. Then she pivoted and skated backward, just out of their reach. As the boy who had threatened me closed in on her, she allowed herself to be backed into the wall. I held my breath, sure he had her, but as her hands touched the wall, she pushed off, stuck out a silky, muscular leg, and tripped him. He was a big boy, and he fell hard on the unforgiving ice.

"You little bitch," he said, staggering to his feet. "I'll get you now."

I gripped the bench beneath me. But Molly was halfway around the rink. She flitted among the skaters, now like a butterfly, quick, iridescent, unpredictable. Finally the boy sliced his way through the teens huddled at the center of the rink and forced her back to the wall. He gripped her shoulders, slashed at her knee with his skate, once, twice, three times, and shot away. Molly took off after him again. When she caught up, she slammed into him, and he fell a second time. His buddies fell on top of him, a tangle of legs and skates and scarves.

Before they got up, Molly flew to the gate and tugged off her skates. "Let's get out of here," she said. Blood streamed down her leg, but she pushed me into the ladies' room, where we retrieved our shoes and dumped our skates.

We ran all the way to her house and collapsed on the steps. "How about a lemonade?" she said. "Then we'd better get down to the theater and ask Mr. Parker what the movie was about." She grinned and picked at the dried blood on her leg.

molly may have been a better skater than me, and more daring, but I outshone her on the basketball court. Not only did I have the height and hands that she did not, but I also had the patience. At recess, I stood on the foul line, shooting basket after basket until I perfected a high and looping swish.

Once when Bobby Baker stole the ball from me on a rebound, Molly taunted him. "Bet she's a better shot than you."

"Oh, yeah?" Bobby dribbled over to the foul line and shoved me aside. "What do you say, best out of ten?" He bounced the ball and gave me a menacing stare.

"You're on," Molly said before I could reply. "I'll keep score." She crossed her arms and stationed herself on the sideline.

I bit a hangnail. Bobby dribbled once, twice, and lofted the ball into the air. It hit the backboard and bounced out of bounds. I retrieved the ball and threw it back to him. His second, third, and fourth shots went cleanly through the net. He missed the next two, made one, missed again, and dropped the last two through the hoop. Six out of ten.

I stepped up to the line and palmed the ball. The first shot was good, also the second and third.

"Hip, hip, hooray!" Molly shouted, high-stepping and clapping like a cheerleader. "Betsy's best any day."

I took the ball again, the dimpled leather rough against my damp hands.

"Look at her choke," Bobby called out.

I shot and missed. The blood pounded in my head. This was my chance to show Molly I was worthy of her admiration.

The next ball circled and bobbled on the rim before falling

away from the basket. I blew the next shot completely—the ball sailed over the backboard.

"Bet-sy, Bet-sy," Molly chanted.

I stepped to the line and sunk the last four balls. Seven out of ten.

Molly rushed over and raised my arm. "And our shoot-out champion, Betsy Thurmont, retains her title." She stuck out her tongue at Bobby.

I had done it.

the following year, we saw the boys with new eyes. We were in sixth grade, and I basked in the spell Molly cast, conscious of their eyes roaming over her braids and legs, like the fingers of the blind—greedy and awestruck.

I was still in love with Molly, too, but there was tension between us. It started over Tommy DiFelice. At fourteen, he had flunked sixth grade three times and was the oldest student in our class. Still, all the girls were crazy about him, but he had eyes only for Molly.

The night of the Teachers-Charleston football game, Molly took me beneath the bleachers on the Charleston side, where we wouldn't be spotted by any teachers or parents who might tell our mothers. She sat on the yellowed grass and drew a packet of cigarettes from the pocket of her purse. I had never smoked, but I watched, enthralled, as she extracted a cigarette, put it between her lips, and lit it with a match. She held it elegantly between her index and middle finger, blowing the smoke skyward into the stands.

She offered the cigarette to me, but I shook my head. She crossed her legs above the knee and rested her elbow on her thigh. The tip of the cigarette glowed in the dusky air, illuminating the golden hairs on her leg.

"Men like it when you smoke," she said. "It's a terrific way to strike up a conversation. You pull out your cigarette case and then look around for your lighter. They always offer you a light. I've watched Mummy till I've got it down pat." She swung her lower leg back and forth, tapping her foot against the empty air.

"Aren't you going to watch the game?" I asked. I hunched forward toward the field, my arms hugging my knees. I was cold.

"The game," Molly snorted. "The game isn't what we're here for. Be patient." She took another deep drag on her cigarette and closed her eyes, satisfied. She hadn't coughed once since she lit up. I realized she had smoked before.

During halftime, while the two bands marched down the field, white boots shining under the stadium lights, the bass drum throbbing to the beat of "Anchors Away," Tommy DiFelice, dressed in a zippered flannel shirt and rolled-up jeans, sauntered up to us. "Well, well, well," he said, pulling up short in front of Molly. "So you showed up."

"I told you we would," Molly said, tipping her head back and exhaling audibly. The smoke swirled above her head.

I knew nothing about a rendezvous with Tommy. He

crouched down beside her, bangs falling over his eyes. There was something raw and dangerous about him.

"Got a smoke for me?" he asked, grinning.

Molly reached into her pocket and brought out the crushed pack of Lucky Strikes. She held the pack out to him, and he let his fingers run down the length of hers before taking it from her. He pulled a lighter out of his back pocket, cupped a hand over the flame, and sucked on the cigarette until it caught fire.

"Thanks," he said, handing the pack back to her, again letting his fingers brush across hers. "I'll see you later."

She nodded. Then he was gone, but the scent of him, smoky and forbidding, remained, wrapped around us like a cloak.

"Molly, have you lost your senses?" I said. "What was that all about?" I was disturbed by the vision of them together, heads almost touching.

"Don't worry," she said. "This is going to be fun." Her foot jiggled furiously, stirring up invisible currents in the damp night air.

The players returned to the field. The colors of their uniforms blurred and ran. I had no idea who was winning.

Then it was over. Charleston had won. I realized that only because of the roar from the bleachers above me.

Molly was already at the gate, calling to me. Her words floated silently on the tidal wave of noise.

"We should go home," I said when I reached her.

"You go home if you want," she said, one hand on her hip.

"But what if Tommy does something?"

"Like what? What's he going to do? Come on."

She turned and plunged into the crowd. I followed. We were nearly separated in the flood of people washing down from the stands, onto the playing field, and out into the night.

I knew I would follow her. I always followed her. And somewhere deep inside, I knew I wanted something—something I couldn't even name—to happen.

She took me to the Teachers bonfire site at the edge of town. A few embers still glowed in the dark as if we'd invaded the remains of a village ransacked and burned only hours before. An immense silence rolled across the land, sweeping closer and engulfing us. Before us stretched harvested cornfields, their brown, flattened stalks like fallen soldiers.

Oblivious to the omens around us, Molly stood, arms crossed, surveying the bonfire's remains.

"You gather some wood," she said. "We need to get this fire going again. See"—she pointed to the vague shapes of tangled branches and makeshift log seats strewn across the trampled grass—"there." Then she knelt before the remains of the fire and coaxed the coals back to life with the remains of her cigarettes.

The night had grown colder. My breath floated, diffident and pale, before me, and my ears burned. When I gathered as many limbs in my arms as I could, I turned my back to the night and returned to Molly.

She took the branches from me and began arranging them

in log-cabin fashion above the tiny flames leaping from the crinkled paper. Then she sat cross-legged on the ground and brought out a bag of marshmallows from beneath her jacket.

I held my palms out to the fire. "We shouldn't be here," I said.

Molly leaned back on her elbows and gazed at the stars. The Seven Sisters flickered overhead.

"When I turn thirteen," she said, "I'm running away from home."

"Where will you go?" I asked.

"Hollywood," she said. "I'm going to be the next National Velvet."

I smoothed my jacket out beside hers and lay on my back. Her assurance eased my fear; I relaxed in the warmth of the fire.

I must have fallen asleep. When I woke, I heard Molly and Tommy whispering from the opposite side of the fire. I hadn't heard his motorcycle, but I saw it leaning on its kickstand a few feet away. He must have walked it the last half mile at least. I would have heard it otherwise.

I lay still, watching them through lowered lashes.

Tommy was leaning on one elbow, head in his hand, inches from Molly's lap. He was whispering, but I couldn't make out what he was saying.

Molly toyed with the end of her braid, tossed it over her shoulder, looked out across the fields. He rolled over on his back, put his head in her lap.

Molly sat very still and gazed off across the charcoal land-scape. I felt as if she had gone somewhere—not in time or space, but in skin and blood and bone—without me.

Tommy took her hand and placed it on his jeans.

"Gosh, I'm starved," Molly said. Her voice shattered the spell of the night. "Come on, Tommy, get up. Let's roast marsh-mallows." She retrieved her hand from his pants, pushed him off her lap, and began rummaging around for a stick.

Tommy looked dazed.

"Here," she said and handed him a stick. She pierced a marshmallow with her own stick and held it over the coals at the edge of the fire. Its smooth, white surface grew bronze and swollen, releasing a sticky sweetness into the atmosphere.

I sat up, unthinking.

"Hey," Molly said, grinning at me through the flames. "You woke up in time for the fun. Grab a stick." She threw a marsh-mallow at me. It sailed through the fire and landed on my jacket. I picked it up and felt around on the ground for a stick.

"Roast your marshmallow, you goon," Molly said to Tommy.

"Nah," Tommy said. "I've got to meet some guys." He stood up and brushed off his backside.

"You don't know what you're missing," Molly said. She popped her marshmallow in her mouth and licked her fingers one at a time.

"I've got to go," Tommy said again. He had lost his strut and swagger, and he turned toward his bike. But Molly caught up with him, grabbed his hand, and whispered something in his ear. Then he straddled his motorcycle and kicked the starter. The bike growled and whined. Tommy popped the clutch and spattered the ground with dirt in his wake. We listened until the roar of the engine was swallowed up by the night.

"He's nuts about me," Molly said.

She never told me what she whispered to Tommy that night. And I never told my mother what I'd seen.

But something changed between us. Molly had a life in which I had no part.

The next weekend, she abandoned me at the fair to ride the Ferris wheel with Tommy. I was forced to share a gondola with two sweaty Boy Scouts whose hands and mouths were sticky with caramel corn. When Molly and Tommy got off, hand in hand, she flirted with the ride attendant and pointed at my gondola, swaying back and forth, the Scouts nudging me with their elbows. The attendant started the ride up again and launched us to the very top of the Ferris wheel, where he brought the ride to an abrupt halt. Molly and Tommy stood far below us, laughing and smoking.

After the incident at the fair, I ignored Molly and linked arms with Sally Swanson every day at recess. Sally's mother was a member of the Daughters of the American Revolution, and we paraded past Molly, noses in the air.

"My mom," Sally said in a confidential tone meant to be overheard, "says some women don't deserve to be called ladies. She says you can tell them right off because of the vulgar way they spill out of their dresses and wear too much lipstick. And of course, most of them got off to the wrong start when they were girls. Too forward with the boys." She patted her skirt, which fell primly to her knees, and sniffed at Molly, whose blue gingham pinafore barely grazed mid-thigh.

But it did not last. After two weeks, I found Sally's virtue suffocating. And she had no sense of fun. She liked to serve tea to her collection of blond-haired, blue-eyed dolls, while the dolls conducted imaginary conversations in which they disparaged their less patrician sisters—whose white gloves were always soiled and whose lineage was smirched with scandal.

When Molly and I made up, we celebrated by snipping a few threads from the buttons of Sally's blouse while she was in gym class so that when she stretched her arms into the sleeves of her coat at the end of the day, all the buttons popped off, exposing her pale chest and her great-great-grandmother's gold cross to her snickering classmates.

"Some girls," Molly mimicked in my ear, "don't deserve to be called ladies. You can tell because they're forever exposing themselves to boys."

That afternoon, she wheedled a motorcycle ride around the schoolyard for both of us from Tommy. I had never had my arms around a boy. Legs wrapped around his, I held on for my life as he kicked the bike into gear, revved the engine, and wove in and out around the playground equipment and basketball standards.

"Relax," he shouted. "Lean into the curves."

But I had turned to petrified wood, unable to enjoy the ride till after it was over, when my legs buckled beneath me and collapsed on a picnic table. Molly straddled the bike and gripped Tommy with her slim legs. She thrust her hands above her head as if she were on a roller-coaster ride.

"Look, Ma, no hands!" she called to me as they whizzed by.

"Who wants to be a lady," she said as we walked home afterward on unsteady legs, "if it means being a drip like Sally? Didn't the motorcycle ride give you the most swell shivers?" She spun in a circle, arms outstretched like airplane wings. "Hey, Tommy!" she called and blew him a kiss as he roared down the street.

That night in bed, images and sensations washed over me and dragged me under. I dreamed I was on Tommy's motorcycle again, my bare legs against his stiff jeans, my blouse unbuttoned and my chest against his T-shirt, his shoulder blades pressing into my skin. "Lean into the curves," he called, and I did, my body melting into his until our clothing dissolved and we rode naked through the streets, waving to the kids outside the sweet shop. Tommy's hair smelled of cigarettes, and I inhaled the smoky fragrance along with the fumes from his bike. We rode on and on, out of town, down dirt roads between rows of corn until the bike itself dissolved into the air. Still, we rode, our bodies pressed together, our legs gripping an invisible, pulsing presence beneath us.

$\mathcal{A}$ the summer before we entered seventh grade, Molly and I were inseparable. She was fickle in her devotion to

Tommy, but constant in her affection for me. Almost every weekend, we stayed at her house or at mine.

Then one Friday, Mrs. Liddell took us out for dinner at a fancy restaurant. "We're celebrating," she said as the waiter handed us our menus. "I have a surprise for you."

She ordered a glass of champagne for herself and ginger ales for Molly and me.

"Here's to the future," she said, raising her glass.

We raised ours as well, uncertain but hopeful. Mrs. Liddell closed her eyes and sipped her champagne as if it had the power to take her to fairyland.

"Well," Molly said, "are you going to tell us, Mum?" She propped her elbows on the table, chin on her folded hands, and waited.

Mrs. Liddell opened her eyes. "Molly, how many times have I told you—elbows off the table. Let's order first, then I'll break the news." She ordered filet mignon for all of us, complete with baked potatoes smothered in butter and sour cream. "We'll have strawberry parfaits for dessert," she told the waiter, handing him the menus as if she were the queen offering him her hand.

"Now," she said when he'd gone. "Guess what?" She looked at me rather than Molly. "We're moving to Ithaca, New York," she said. "Good-bye, dreary Charleston."

I sat stunned and paralyzed. Perhaps it was a joke.

But Mrs. Liddell didn't laugh.

Beside me, Molly balled up her napkin and threw it on the

table. "I hate you," she said. "You're a wicked, horrid mother, and I'm not going with you. I'm staying with Betsy."

But of course, Molly had no choice. She had to go. They left a week later. It was so sudden I had no time to acclimate myself to what was happening.

Our last night together, Molly and I took a bath, our hair floating around us like seaweed.

"We should hold a ceremony," Molly said. She raised one pink and slippery leg and stretched out her toes to touch the tub's metal spout.

"What do you mean?" I rested my head against hers, admiring her leg. I cupped a handful of iridescent bubbles and blew on them, setting the oily blue and purple swirls into motion.

"An initiation ceremony," Molly said. Her voice was lazy but solemn. "You know, like the Indians do."

"Like what Indians do?" I asked.

Molly's knowledge of other cultures was muddied, like her mother's—she was an erratic student, not because she wasn't bright but because her mind skipped across dates and facts like stones across water—but the idea of a ceremony intrigued me. I wanted something to seal our friendship and mark this night.

After we dried off, back in my room we set the alarm for midnight. The curtains hung limp, and outside a dove cooed from its perch in the old, scarred maple into which we'd carved our names. Despite the heat, I snuggled close to Molly. She tucked her head beneath my chin, her hair damp and lilac-scented. Usually we chattered beneath the sheets or tickled each other till we collapsed in exhaustion, but that night we were silent, listening to the night. Even after my fingers grew numb, I lay still, letting Molly doze in the crook of my arm.

We must have fallen asleep like that, for we awoke to the dull bleat of the alarm, muffled beneath the pillow so my mother and father wouldn't hear. Molly snapped on a flashlight and swung her legs over the edge of the bed. She stuffed a towel under the door to stifle the light and sound, then opened her mother's makeup kit, which she'd stolen, while I rummaged in the closet for my sewing basket. We folded a blanket on the floor and arranged our pillows on either end. Next we sat cross-legged, facing each other, our knees just touching. Molly took her mother's lipstick and drew a red stripe down my nose. She took the dark blue eye pencil and made three slashes across each of my cheeks, her fingers moving like feathers over my face.

It was my turn. I took the tube of lipstick in my hand and uncapped it. It was cool against my fingers, and I leaned toward Molly, put one hand under her chin, and with the other traced a stripe down her nose. She smiled.

I picked up the pencil and used the thumb of my left hand to pull her skin taut. With my right hand, I drew the slashes, one beneath the other, across her cheeks. She grabbed the mirror and inspected herself.

"We look like Injuns," she said. She put down the mirror and picked up the matches. "Get a needle."

Molly lit a match and held the flame to the tip of the needle I held out till it glowed red. She blew out the match and held out her left hand, palm up.

"Here," she said, pointing to her wrist. "Prick me here, till it bleeds."

She sat motionless while I held her hand and selected a vein. It was a slender thread of robin's egg blue. I touched the tip of the needle to her skin, clenched my teeth, and jabbed.

"Good," Molly said. Three drops of blood bloomed on her wrist.

Molly took the needle. I gave her my arm, upturned like a sacrifice. The sharp steel pricked my skin. I gasped.

"Open your eyes," she said.

She clasped my hand and bound a ribbon around our wrists. "Blood sisters," she said.

"Blood sisters," I repeated, gripping her fingers.

We closed our eyes, our wrists still bound together. Bursts of reds and blues and purples exploded on the inner surface of my eyelids. I could no longer tell where Molly ended and I began. I swam inside her veins, felt her course through me as if we had become our very blood itself.

When we said good-bye the next morning, I had no idea I would never see her again.

part two

i have never had another friendship like that I had with Molly. One loves only once with such intensity and devotion. Yet I long for that lost love, at once innocent and self-assured. I long to renew our oath of blood, to say, "I will not forsake you."

Did I forsake her, or she, me? Was there any other course our friendship might have taken? Sometimes I think I would have rather had a violent break, our love affirmed in the heat of anger.

Instead, we merely grew apart.

I suppose it might have happened even had Molly remained in Charleston. I suppose there might have been more fights over Tommy DiFelice or other boys. I suppose one day Molly might have decided that I was much too shy and tame, or perhaps I would have found the bravado that I once thought thrilling had become merely rash.

I long. I wonder. I suppose. But I cannot change what was, what is.

Molly died. And I am left with only memories and her diaries.

What happened was this: Molly moved away. We wrote, we wrote less often, we no longer wrote at all.

I grew unfaithful to her memory.

I forgot the rush and spark I'd felt when she orchestrated some outrageous escapade. I forgot I had defended her when rumors of her mother's indiscretions rippled through the classroom. Instead, as stories of Mrs. Liddell's transgressions multiplied, I distanced myself from Molly, claimed I, too, had always known she'd become as reckless as her mother. I began to think it was good fortune she had left. After Lieutenant Johnson stuck a shotgun in his mouth and blew his brains out, a note to Molly's mother in his pocket, I knew it was.

And yet.

And yet I could not forget how lovely Molly's mother was, how lovely Molly was herself. I could not forget how much I wished that I, too, could kindle such a passion.

I was torn between forgetting and remembering, until with time the past became a dream.

Then, my senior year in high school, Molly wrote.

Saturday, November 29, 1952

Dear Betsy,

I'll bet you don't even remember me!
Molly, your blood sister! Do you remember
the night before Mum and I left for
Ithaca? Well, I'm in Denver, Colorado, now
(not Hollywood!), and I'm MARRIED. Can
you believe it?

Mum died five years ago. It's a long
story. She got married, too, right before she
died. I lived with my stepfather for a while,
then I was on my own. Now Bob (my
husband) and I are expecting a baby.

Which is why I'm writing. Betsy, do you
remember the night we pledged we'd do
anything for each other? Please promise to
be my baby's godmother.

I do hope you remember me, Betsy, and
I do hope you'll say yes. I know we've lost
touch, and I know it must seem strange, me
writing to you now like this.

Please, Betsy, don't let me down. It
would mean so much. I'm naming her after

you. Elizabeth means "consecrated to God," did you know that? Molly means "wished-for child," which is ridiculous, of course, because Mum would have rather had a boy, but so what? My daughter will be "wished for." Dick, my stepdad, gave Bob and me a bundle of money last month so we could buy a house. Bob's family lives in Denver, right across the street in fact. Little Betsy will have a grandmother and grandfather and aunts and uncles to spoil her, and I suppose she'll be as rude to me as I was to poor Mum.

You probably wonder why, then, I'm asking you to be her godmother with so many doting relatives willing to take the job. Betsy, I want her to know about her other grandparents, too. I want her to know about Daddy. And even Mummy. You can tell her. Please promise me you will.

Do write. I don't have any girlfriends here yet, although Bob's mom is super. And do tell me about everything. I hope you haven't forgotten me. Maybe little Betsy and I will visit you one day, and you must come and visit us. I want her to know her namesake.

Well, Bob will be home from work soon, and I've got to get us some dinner. My back aches, and you should see me waddle around the kitchen with my huge belly. I wish the baby would come tomorrow. Every night, I rub my stomach and tell her stories about us. She doesn't kick as much then. I think she likes stories.

So do I. So please, please, write and tell me how you are, and please say you'll be her godmother. (Have I begged pathetically enough?)

Love,
Your long-lost Molly
(Mrs. Robert Porter!)

Wednesday, December 10, 1952

DEAR MOLLY,

I was overwhelmed to get your letter. Of course I still remember you. And of course I'd be thrilled to be little Betsy's godmother.

Molly, dear, I'm so sorry about your mother.

Mom and Dad send their love and sympathy, too. We are all praying for you and your family. Mom says be sure to eat right— you know Mom! And Dad says if you don't have an attorney, he can help you with your will. He says you must draw up a will if you are going to have a baby.

Isn't it odd, we never played with dolls, and now you're going to have the real thing. Are you scared? I would be. But then, you were never afraid of anything. When is the baby due?

Molly, do write again and tell me everything. What about your stepfather? Are you still in touch with him?

My life is not nearly as eventful. I'm a starting forward on the basketball team this year. Last season we won the league championship, and I scored an average sixteen points per game. Leonelle Trilling's on the team, too. Do you remember her? She goes by "Nelly" now.

I hope to go to the University of Chicago in the fall and then on to Harvard for a law degree, like Dad. I'm helping out in his office on Saturdays—mostly typing and filing, but I'm learning a lot. When I'm finished, I read through his case books. It's fascinating.

Mom and Dad say to let us know if we can do anything else.

We want the best for you and wish you and your husband a
blessed Christmas.

Love,

Betsy

molly never wrote back.

Then, in early January, my father received a call from a Denver law firm. I was at a slumber party at Nelly's when he phoned to give me the news. I listened with difficulty, as if to a radio program plagued by static.

"—died New Year's Eve," he said.

I clutched the phone, while from the bedroom came shrieks of laughter. I put a finger to my other ear. Outside, snow was falling. I wanted to be that snow, numb and white.

The girls ended their pillow fight and spilled out into the living room.

"—traveling to Colorado next week," my father said.

From the living room my friends sang along with Patti Page, "How much is that doggie in the window?"

"Can I go with you?" I asked.

"No, it'll be a long trip, and a fast one. I'll give you a full report. I'm sorry, Betsy. I know how much you loved her. Your mother and I did, too. We can arrange for a memorial service here in Charleston when I get back."

"I want to go with you." I continued to stare out the window. The snow was falling faster now, fast and silent, transforming shrubs and bushes into surreal and random burial mounds.

My mother got on the phone. "Sweetheart, I'm so sorry." Her voice was thick, as if she'd been crying. "Try to be strong. Molly's with God now."

The sound of "Shine, little glow worm" had replaced Patti Page, and my friends had lined up like dancers from the Moulin Rouge and were high-kicking across the room, breathless and laughing.

"Come get me," I said to my mother. "I can't stay here."

Molly was dead. Molly was dead. Molly was dead.

She had died giving birth to a stillborn daughter on New Year's Eve, while my friends and I were singing "Auld Lang Syne." Her husband hanged himself the next day.

Two days later, my father, his eyes heavy and lined, handed me a box filled with Molly's diaries and mementos and a glass-topped wooden case in which were ranged rows of butterflies, pale blue and yellow, soft brown, and brilliant orange and cobalt. "She wanted you to have these," he said. "It was in her will."

I took her treasures to my room. The butterflies seemed to flutter in their coffin, at once restless and at peace. I found I could not contemplate them for long. I put the case on my bookshelf and turned to Molly's box, which was covered in moss-green wrapping paper sprigged with violets. How many times had Molly removed the lid, as I was doing now? How often had she added to its contents?

I had a box, too, although mine was patterned with lilies of the valley. Over the years, I had added Christmas cards and valentines from friends (Molly would have been eighteen on Valentine's Day), the church bulletin from my confirmation, brochures from my mother's exhibitions, a photograph of our championship basketball team, playbills and movie tickets, and, in the bottom, the long-ago letters and postcards from Molly.

I had never kept a journal. Now it seemed a mistake. If someone were to read the scraps of paper in my box, would they tell anything about my life? What would Molly's box reveal to me?

On top lay the letter I'd written to Molly less than a month ago. How trivial it seemed now, how shallow. Beneath it were her diaries, a stack of postcards and photographs, some faded clippings.

I opened the first of Molly's journals. The inscription read, "From Miss Elizabeth Anne Thurmont to Miss Mary Alice Liddell" next to a photo of Dorothy Lamour in long black gloves which I'd cut from a movie magazine. The first entry, in Molly's looping hand, read:

"I will never forgive Mummy for taking me away from Betsy. At least she let me stay at Betsy's house last night—she said I'd be in the way while she finished packing, but I know Lieutenant Johnson came to help her. I heard her talking on the phone.

Betsy and I are blood sisters now—so we can't ever forget each other or let each other down, no matter what, no matter where we are."

I could not read on.

I went downstairs, clinging to the railing. "Mom," I said, "I can't go to the game tonight. I can't play." I had never missed a practice, much less a game.

"Are you sick?" My mother looked up from her darning.

"No. Yes. I don't know." My throat felt tight, my head light. "I need to go for a walk."

"Is it about Molly, dear?" She took off her glasses and held out her arms.

"It's not about anything. I don't want to talk."

I felt prickly, like a porcupine. I did not want anyone to hold me. I left the house without my coat.

I walked and walked and walked, willing the cold to invade my lungs, to stop my heart. I had told my mother nothing when it might have made a difference. I could not tell her now how I had watched Molly become more like her mother—how she flirted with Tommy DiFelice just as Mrs. Liddell flirted with Mr. Parker, with the veterans. I had a premonition about the diaries. Something terrible, something I might have prevented. Now it was too late.

On a lane through the woods outside town, I came upon an oak. Halfway up, its trunk was swollen and blistered, as by an infestation or a blight. Then the tree rose straight and tall again.

I wanted to be like that oak, to wear a scar on my body to mark this day.

"Here," I wanted to say, "this is where I bled. This is where I lost her."

At last the tears came. I don't know how long I walked or where, only that when I returned home, my cheeks were crusted with frozen, salty streaks and I felt both hot and chilled at once.

I lay in bed for two weeks. I would miss the height of the basketball season, but I no longer cared. I devoured Molly's diaries, my guilt intensifying with every page I read.

Wednesday, July 10, 1946

Dear diary:

I said good-bye to Betsy today. . . . Everything I love is either back in Charleston or on the moving van, some-where ahead of us on the way to New York. The posters of Alan Ladd and Veronica Lake in _This Gun for Hire_ that Mr. Parker gave me, all my clothes except two pairs of underpants, a clean pair of jeans, and my sailor outfit (powder blue—midriff—you can see my belly button!), which I packed in my pink valise with the little mirror in the lid. Mummy made me give my blue bike to the Salvation Army—my last birthday present from Daddy.

"You're too big to ride it," she said. "Don't be selfish, Molly. Think of the children whose families can't afford to buy them bicycles. Think of how difficult you're making this for me. You're not the only one leaving things behind."

"Yes," I wanted to say, "but no one's running me out of town."

One day I'll be on my own and do whatever I please. I'll be like Veronica Lake and dance and sing, "I've got you right where I wanted you—dangling on my line—'cause I'm not yours; you're mine." I'll perform magic tricks, too, and go home every night with the handsomest man in the room. I never would have married that dreadful copper boyfriend. I'd never marry anyone who said, "Look, sugar, what would it take to get you to darn my socks?" Not me. I'll marry a man who doesn't care about darned socks and made beds. Instead, we'll hop trains and track down spies selling secrets to the Japanese.

Mummy has been so hot under the collar. She didn't allow me to bring a single comic or movie magazine. Finally she agreed I could read the book of Emily Dickinson's poems that Mrs.

Thurmont gave me QUIETLY in the car.

"None of that mad laughter, Molly,"
she said this afternoon. "You are a young
lady, not a hyena. Please try to behave
like one."

I put my head back and howled.

"Mary Alice Liddell, that's enough.
I ought to put you out by the side of the
road." She glared at me. "No wonder
men don't look at me twice. Who'd want
a stepdaughter like you?"

"You shouldn't frown so much, Mummy.
You're beginning to get wrinkles," I said
s-o-l-i-c-i-t-o-u-s-l-y. Betsy and I find a
new word in the dictionary each week.
That was last week's. Mum was furious. Oh,
how I shall miss Betsy.

We are staying at a rinky-dink motel
in the middle of NOWHERE tonight.
Mummy is taking a long bath, to soothe
her nerves.

"What I put up with for you," she said.
"If you had the slightest idea how much I
sacrifice on your behalf."

74   nancy j. jones

Thursday, July 11, 1946

I'm writing tonight from Pittsburgh, which is HUGE compared to Charleston, and has three rivers—the Allegheny and Monongahela, which run together and become the Ohio. There are great steel mills belching clouds of smoke and soot, and Mum won't take me to ride the Duquesne incline, which looks like a railroad car with one end on stilts and carries people up and down a steep hill. We can't take the trolley, either. Who knows what kinds of folks ride public transportation here, she says. Plus, the air is so DIRTY! But it didn't stop her from putting on her white dress, the one with only one shoulder, and her white sandals for dinner. She's meeting our waiter—doesn't he look like Cary Grant, she says—for drinks right now.

So here I am cooped up in this room while Mum has all the fun. I am so bored. I wish Betsy were here. We could order hot fudge sundaes from room service. The man in uniform who runs the elevator (brass rails and a mirror in which Mum retouched her lipstick) reads the Phantom, too. He loaned me the newest issue.

Mum made me throw out all my old comics before we left. She has been a stinker about everything. Now that Daddy is dead—already two years—she says we must put the past behind us, begin a new life. She will be a "career girl"—a secretary or receptionist—and earn her own money, and I'll go to the "best schools." She says we will find more "culture" in New York.

What she means is no one will know us there.

What she means is we must forget about Daddy. I hate her for that.

I will never forget him. I will never forget Betsy.

Betsy and I heard her mom say to her dad that we're moving because of what happened with Lieutenant Johnson, the time the police found him drunk, crying on our front door step and beating on the door with his cane.

"Not to mention Lowell Parker," Mrs. Thurmont said. "It's a wonder his wife hasn't thrown him out."

"You disloyal little girl," Mum said when I asked her about it. "You can't possibly know how much you've wounded me. A good-looking woman is always a target for gossip. You learn to ignore it," she said. "You hold your head up and move on—which is that much harder when your own daughter is against you."

I told her I was not against her, that I liked Lieutenant Johnson and Mr. Parker, too, but she said we would not discuss it ever again.

So we are off to Ithaca, New York, where we will live in Grandma Liddell's old house. Daddy got his first biology degree at Cornell University, Mummy said. I hope Ithaca has a good theater. The Will Rogers in Charleston is swell—red velvet curtains, lights running down the aisle so you can find your seat in the dark—and, of course, Mr. Parker used to let us in for free.

"I know how hard it is for a widow to raise a child," he used to say to Mummy.

"You're a fine-looking woman, ma'am, don't take offense," he told her once. "If you'll excuse me for saying so, Rita Hayworth doesn't have a thing on you. Why, if you were a ranch, you'd be the Bar None."

That was the time we went to see Gilda. Then he walked us home, like he always did. I don't see why it was such a big deal.

Mrs. Simpson at church called Mummy a tramp. I was in the toilet stall in the bathroom off the fellowship hall. Mrs. Simpson came in with Mrs. Davenport. Old biddies.

"Did you see that dress Catherine is wearing?" Mrs. Simpson said. I could picture her huffing and dabbing at her cheeks. "And her husband not a year in his grave. When she bends over to pour the coffee, you can see the top of her brassiere. No doubt the only reason she's on the social committee. And I'll never forget that getup she wore at the V-J Day Parade last year. Sitting on the hood of a car dressed like Uncle Sam and her leg draped over some soldier's. The poor child. No father and an unfit mother. If she turns out well, it will be a modern-day miracle."

Hmph! Mummy may be a pill, but she's right. Mrs. Simpson's jealous!

I will be glamorous, too, when I'm grown up and go out with a lot of men. They will take me to dinner, and I will order only the most expensive items on the menu. _En français_. I am so glad Betsy's Grandma Keckler taught us French. I will live in Paris, like she did, and meet someone like Humphrey Bogart.

A molly's diary entries that first year in Ithaca cataloged a list of grievances against her mother, combined with a growing defiance of Mrs. Liddell's mandates. Whatever bond mother and daughter had managed to construct after Dr. Liddell died eroded as they traveled East and disintegrated completely not long after they moved into the drafty, old row house in Ithaca.

Mrs. Liddell refused to buy Molly a new bicycle. Molly responded by purchasing one herself with money she earned raking leaves. She rode to Cornell University, where she flirted with the young men on campus every chance she got.

Mrs. Liddell insisted Molly take piano rather than voice lessons. Molly retaliated by playing "Chopsticks" and "Heart and Soul" over and over until her mother forbade her to touch the instrument again.

By Molly's twelfth birthday, Mrs. Liddell refused to throw her daughter any party whatsoever and left her with a neighboring spinster while Mrs. Liddell herself traveled to New York City to celebrate Valentine's Day in the Starlight Room of the Waldorf Astoria with a stockbroker who promised to find her work on Wall Street. Molly struck back once again with the seam ripper she'd used to detach Sally's buttons, this time snipping a few threads in the seat of her mother's slacks, so that over time, Mrs. Liddell's satin underpants peeked through the seams as she knelt in the garden or, once, when the stockbroker was up from the city, as she bent to poke the fire.

While Mrs. Liddell never connected her split seams with her

daughter, their fights grew more explosive and Molly spent more and more nights at the home of her new friend Christine, whom she had met at dance lessons that summer. Christine's mother had lived in London for the past five years, and her father, abandoned by his wife, showered Christine with sapphires and pearls. He arranged for summer vacations at their estate in the Hamptons, to which Molly was invited, professional photography sessions for a modeling portfolio to send to the agencies in New York City.

When I first saw Christine's photograph, my heart stopped. At eighteen, I was already what my mother called "solid." I stood five feet, eleven inches, in my bare feet, taller than most of the boys in my class, and I could palm a basketball in one hand.

Christine, in contrast, was, even at twelve, svelte and elegant. She wore a sleeveless satin evening gown and over-the-elbow gloves. Her dark hair plunged down her back in a torrent of waves, and her lips parted in carmine allure. She had signed the photo in a generous, flowing hand, "Molly, hugs and kisses! Love, Chrissy," and I realized with a jolt that just as I had replaced Molly with sensible Leonelle Trilling, so had she replaced me with a far more exotic companion, one whose adventures made Molly's antics in Charleston seem tame. In the Hamptons, Molly and Chrissy met two boys at the beach. After Molly turned her ankle playing volleyball, one of the boys carried her all the way to Chrissy's house, where he brought her lemonade and massaged her stockinged foot. Back in Ithaca, the girls sat in the back of the movie theater and necked with high-school boys who slid their hands beneath the girls' blouses and caressed their breasts so that, Molly said, "I felt all light and floaty inside, as if I had the most thrilling fever."

On Christine's thirteenth birthday, the girls helped themselves to a bottle of Christine's father's Dom Perignon, which when they opened it, exploded with such force the cork dented the kitchen ceiling and fizzy champagne rained down on them.

"We licked each other's fingers," Molly wrote, "and then poured ourselves two fluty crystal glasses each. We got so dizzy, and Christine said I must pretend to be her boyfriend and kiss her. She showed me how men and women kiss, flicking their tongues in and out of each other's mouths. I felt as if I were all lit up inside, but the next morning, I had a dreadful headache."

When I first read these entries, I remembered summer mornings, the world still shrouded in a hazy yellow fog, when we played hide-and-seek and Molly's skin flushed pink and perspired above her upper lip and along her arms and legs like roses beaded with dew. I remembered muggy evenings, too, the moonlight falling across my bed and Molly's minty, vaporous breath as she poured her plans into my ear, sweaty palms against my shoulder, one bent leg carelessly thrown across mine as I lay on my back and drifted on her dreams.

As I read about Christine, I realized how far apart Molly and I had grown and how fast. I realized I had lost her long before she died. My friends and I once shared a bottle of whiskey in the parking lot during a school dance, but I was unnerved by the loss of control over my legs, the stumbling, halting gait that replaced my sure, strong strides. And when my friends and I had slumber parties, our wildest pranks involved short-sheeting one another's beds and painting heavy sleepers' faces with ghoulish makeup.

I still knew little of the "thrilling fever" of which Molly wrote. Even by my senior year, I had never gone steady. I had never even dated.

True, there were the dances at school and at the Grange, but I was so tall the boys almost never asked me to be their partner. Once, when our Tri-Hi-Y organized a hayride, I asked Bobby Baker to be my date. We still challenged each other to foul-shooting contests on the court from time to time, but I was lost without a ball in my hand. We huddled beneath one of Grandma Keckler's quilts, the hay scratchy at our backs, our breath forming vapor trails in the night air. Bobby put a hand inside my coat. I clutched at it, tugged it back to the safe environs of his jacket pocket.

"Grandma made this quilt from scraps of my old dresses," I said to distract him. "This one was my Easter dress when I was six." I pointed to a square of pale yellow calico sprigged with pink roses and then flushed with embarrassment. I sounded inane. Everyone in Charleston had grandmothers who made quilts out of fabric remnants.

"You have nice hands," Bobby said, squeezing mine where it now rested in his pocket. His thumb stroked the back of my hand, slowly, rhythmically, as if he were performing hypnosis.

"They're too big," I said. "But they're okay for basketball."

He might have tried to kiss me that night when he escorted me to my door, but I stuck out my oversized hand and shook his in a firm grip.

"Thanks," I said. "That was fun." How stupid I sounded.

"Well, good night," he said. He was the only boy tall enough to look me in the eye, and he gazed at me for a long time, not letting go of my hand.

"I have to go," I said. "My parents will be waiting up for me." Then I darted through the door.

I felt confident, at home in my body, only on the court, dribbling the ball on the run toward the basket, leaping, twisting, a flick of the wrist, the ball arcing through the air, dropping through the net with a satisfying swish. Then, panting, I wiped the sweat from my eyes and allowed myself the sensation of those early days with Molly.

But I never finished that last season. I never returned to the court again. After two weeks' bed rest, I had not recovered from my illness. My throat was raw and swollen, my joints ached. Still, my heart ached more. I had finished Molly's diaries. Her story seemed both inexplicable and inevitable.

Her diaries reminded me of Anne Frank's, not in their tone, but in their outcome. "It's difficult," Anne wrote less than a month before she was captured, "in times like these: ideals, dreams and cherished hopes rise within us, only to be crushed by grim reality."

Now I faced not only Molly's grim reality, but mine. Dr. Wilson diagnosed rheumatic fever. I was hospitalized. I lay for days in a bed with railings in the children's ward of St. Francis Hospital in Chicago. The children in the other beds coughed and languished. One was dying of a mysterious wasting disease. Her eyes were at once burning and moist, as if she had already had a glimpse of paradise and waited only for that moment when she would draw her last, rasping breath.

Death had never seemed so personal, so close. Molly's brother had been more of a saint than a boy of flesh and blood, her father a devastating but not unlikely tragedy. And the war had been so far away, our sacrifices stirring and heroic. True, Anne had died in Bergen-Belsen, but this was the United States of America, not Nazi Germany. How could Molly die? The girl in the bed beside me?

I was transferred to a private room, green the color of lima beans. Nurses with too-bright smiles and voices took my temperature, my blood, and plumped my pillows. Reverend Farley, bespectacled and hunchbacked, sat beside my bed and read Psalm 23. I thought of Beth in *Little Women*, "Yea, though I walk through the valley of the shadow of death, I will fear no evil."

I, too, might die. I gazed out the window at the dull winter sky, the pale, cold sun. On the windowsill were baskets of flowers and fruit, cards from Nelly Trilling and the rest of the team. Why had I cared so about running across court and tossing a ball through a hoop?

At the end of the season, Nelly came to see me, bringing a silver trophy. "The team decided you should have this," she said, placing it on the table at the foot of my bed.

I don't want it, I thought. I smiled. It was a dreadful effort. How many muscles did it take to smile? Twenty-three?

Unsure of herself, she smiled, too, a half-smile, and rummaged in her pocketbook. "Bobby Baker sent you this." She handed me an envelope.

It was another card. The 23rd Psalm again. They all thought I was going to die.

"I think he's going to ask you to the prom." Nelly folded her hands in her lap.

"We're not in church," I said. "And I don't want to go to the prom."

"I know you must feel dreadful," she said. "Cooped up in this horrible room." She blushed, as if embarrassed that she had blurted out what was better left unsaid.

"I like this room," I said. "I want to stay here all my life. When no one bothers me, I can read all day." I pointed to the stack of books teetering on my nightstand.

"Oh, Betsy," Nelly said, directing her remarks to the wall above me. "You'll get well. You will. We're all praying for you."

But I did not get well.

Grandma Keckler and Mother had moved out of their hotel and were living at a college friend of Mother's in Chicago. They came to see me every day. Grandma darned socks or read from the original French edition of Simone de Beauvoir's *Le deuxième sexe*. Mother read the *Chicago Tribune* or listened to reports of Senator McCarthy's hearings on the radio.

"Hmph," she said. "The only one with any real courage in Washington is Margaret Chase Smith. The rest of them are fools and cowards. It's not Communism they're afraid of—they can't stand the idea of women and workers gaining any power."

She was still seething over Ike's election as president.

But I cared little for anything and paid no attention to her tirades.

For the first time in my life, I had no appetite and had begun to lose weight. To tempt me, Mother and Grandma brought me wonton soup and egg rolls from our favorite Chinese restaurant, the Gold Dragon. I had always loved the fearsome masks and ornate, ivory Chinese characters that adorned the walls, the feel of the smooth, wooden chopsticks in my fingers. I had learned how to use chopsticks when I was seven, when we first visited the Gold Dragon after a trip to Lincoln Park Zoo.

"Mrs. Li sent these specially for you." Mother handed me a cellophane wrapper of fortune cookies. "She said they're for good luck."

I took a sip of the soup, set it down. I had not yet touched my egg roll.

"When can I go home?" I asked.

Mother had won a juried competition at Columbia College the year before. One of the photographs was of Molly and me at ten, sitting on the front steps, heads bent together, knees muddy, examining a salamander we'd found beneath the porch. Mother had brought me a framed five-by-seven print to keep at

my bedside. I could still feel the clammy coldness of the salamander, the light, sticky feel of its feet crawling across my palm.
Now that coldness seemed to creep up my arms, along my skin.

"Next week," she said, smoothing her skirt. "But you won't
be able to go to school. We'll tutor you at home, Grandma and I.
Your heart . . . " Her voice trailed off. "Dr. Wilson will be in to
talk with you soon."

"I don't want to talk to the doctor. I don't want to talk to
anyone ever again." I crumpled the unopened fortune cookies
still in their wrapper.

"Be brave, Betsy." Mother put her hand on mine.

"I don't want to be brave," I said. I pulled my hand back and
buried my face in the pillow. It smelled of bleach and antiseptic,
but nothing could eradicate the odor of foreboding and defeat
that permeated the room.

By dinnertime, I knew the worst. I would live, but my heart
was damaged, the mitral valve unable to properly contract. Even
if I wanted to, I would never sprint up and down the court, ball in
hand, again.

I had my scar, but it gave no satisfaction.

Graduation, college, law school—all these seemed pointless
and absurd.

In the days that followed, I lost myself in books. I wept for
Thomas Hardy's Tess, and, like her, saw the gallows as a respite.
"This happiness could not have lasted. It was too much," she
said before they hanged her.

Perhaps Molly was better off than I. She was, at least, at

peace, whereas I was condemned to live with the knowledge of her fate, with the knowledge that to trust too much, to love too freely, was to be destroyed.

Only Ovid's *Metamorphoses* suggested a solution: Daphne, fleeing from Apollo, finds refuge as a laurel tree; Io, defiled by mighty Jupiter, is transformed into a heifer; Syrinx, faithful only to Diana, becomes the pipes of Pan.

I was tall as a tree, with fingers that spread like branches without leaves, but even this seemed insufficient to protect me. Now my heart had let me down as well.

For my return home, Mother made me a red silk mandarin suit from a pattern Mrs. Li had given her. Two patch pockets at the hem of the jacket were trimmed in gold braid and embroidered with the Chinese characters for "happiness" and "longevity." But I no longer hoped for either.

Saturday, May 24, 1947

Oh, diary!

Can you imagine? Mum's scheme to abandon me for a career on Wall Street seems a positively pregnant idea! You know how blue I've been, imagining Mum there while I'm stranded here in Ithaca! Chrissy has told me all about Broadway. The thought of Mum having all the fun has had me so down in the dumps.

Picture me stuck here with that dreadful Miss Frazier. I'll never forget the time after Michael died when she came to live with us. Oh, diary, you can imagine how dreadful it was, with that woman in the house day and night. She smelled. Then there was the bathroom, with her enema hanging from the showerhead and her stinky old lady's shoes. I had to hold my nose.

Well, diary, Mum planned to LEAVE ME ALONE with that constipated old woman and the new boarder who's renting the spare bedroom.

"A college professor from Massachusetts," she said, "quite the thing for you, Molly, dear. He has the most divine manners and speaks with a British accent. Perhaps you'll learn to speak more civilly to adults. And forgo that dreadful slang you bring home from the movies. Really, Molly, you must learn to express yourself more elegantly. 'That's swell, sister,' is dreadfully common."

You know Mum, the way she flicks her cigarette at the ashtray when she's point—ing out what's wrong with me.

So, you can understand how I loathed, absolument loathed, the thought of the two of them running my life. You can imagine dinner every night. Miss Frazier bustling back and forth from the kitchen, her stockings bunched around her ankles. And at the head of the table where dear Daddy used to sit, Professor Henry Higgins instructing me in etiquette and elocution. Her bowels, his vowels. What a swell summer. Yes, Mum, swell.

But now, can you believe it, that revolting old woman has decided to go live with her sister. Even better, Dr. Richard Richard looks just like Alan Ladd! Wavy, chestnut hair. Dark, brooding eyes. And his trench coat smells of aftershave. He was raised in Paris, because his father was the ambassador to France, so he speaks perfect French! (And that's where he got the British accent, too — boarding school.) I am quite giddy.

I saw the way he looked at me when Mum introduced me. You know how she tries to dismiss me when there are good-looking men around. Well, it was one of those beastly hot days, and I was rocking on the porch swing, drinking lemonade and reading a magazine when there he was. I was wearing my red polka-dot top and blue shorts. I lowered my sunglasses and stared at him. And he stared right back at me. As if I were a hot fudge sundae. I pushed my toes against the floorboards to make the swing rock faster, and he never took his eyes off my legs. I had the most wonderful chills running up and down my spine. I forgot completely how horrid and hot it was.

Oh, this will be such fun. If only Mum doesn't spoil it. She has canceled her plans to move to New York City. So much for the stockbroker.

Tuesday, June 10, 1947

Dick is thirty-five. I asked him at breakfast yesterday.

I brought him tea and toast with marmalade and batted my eyes at him. He's definitely gaga about me. Mum would be furious if she knew. She has been such a wet blanket since he arrived.

After he finishes teaching the summer term at Cornell, he's going on a book tour for his latest novel, _Hunting in the Enchanted Forest_. I would give anything to go with him. A real AUTHOR!

Chrissy says older men make the best beaus.

"Let him know you're interested," she said. "Find a reason to sit close to him. And kiss him, for heaven's sakes, kiss him, the way I taught you."

Chrissy is going to camp this summer. I don't think I could stand being left behind if it weren't for Dick.

Mum fusses at me every time I so much as stop to see what he's reading or WALK BY. "Don't annoy our guest, Molly," she said this morning, flicking the dish towel at me. "He can hardly be amused by the antics of a schoolgirl."

If only she knew the way he touched my leg last while we sat on the porch. Like a feather. It gave me goosebumps.

I have taken to pelting him with balled-up socks and towels. That should get his attention. Besides, it is great fun and it infuriates crummy Mummy to no end.

Friday, June 20, 1947

Oh, diary, you'll never believe what happened. I spent the morning in paradise, and then I was kicked out.

Mum took back her promise to go on a picnic today. Simply because Mrs. Harvey's daughter Sharon is sick. Actually, Sharon is not sick at all. She said her mother thinks it scandalous for Mum and me to be living with an unmarried boarder. And a novelist at that. People are beginning to talk, she said.

Just like before.

Except they are wrong, because Dick likes _me_.

So instead of the three of us going on a picnic, Mum went shopping for a gown. She is sure that Dr. Richard will ask her to the chancellor's summer "Moonlight and Roses" evening garden party, and she simply cannot wear something homemade.

"Your behavior is unacceptable," she said

before she left. "If you think you're going to behave like this—after all I've done for you—you are quite mistaken. It's intolerable. I won't have it."

"Your behavior is unacceptable. It's quite intolerable," I mimicked.

"Don't think you're going to get away with this, Miss High and Mighty!" said mean old Mum, and she slammed the door on the way out.

After she left, I went to her bedroom and stole her favorite lipstick. It's a lovely red, so I tried some on in the bathroom. Then I put on my navy blue sailor outfit, which shows off my tummy. Dick was in the living room rustling the newspaper, so I thumped downstairs on my behind and pretended to trip over the coffee table and fall into his lap.

"Oops," I said, batting my eyes at him. "Sorry about your newspaper, Professor." I rolled onto the floor and giggled. "Gee, I'm hungry. Want a peach, Dick Tracy? Be a peach, Molly, and get us a peach, why don't you? Gosh, Molly, what a peachy keen idea." I hiccuped and sashayed out to the kitchen. Dick coughed and smoothed out his newspaper.

When I got back to the living room, I lounged against the door frame and threw a peach to Dick. "Hey, Professor, catch!" It smacked against the paper and fell to the floor. "You dope," I said.

Then I sauntered over and sat down beside him. "Do you know how to eat a peach?" I asked.

Dick FINALLY folded his paper and put it on the table. "No," he said, "I suspect I don't, but I suppose you're going to show me."

"Of course," I said. "I wouldn't want you to offend the chancellor by eating one the wrong way at the next university picnic." I've practiced eating peaches. I tipped my head back and closed my eyes and brought it to my lips. It's important to have a juicy one. You nip at the skin, take just the tiniest bite so that the juice runs down your fingers. Then you lick it off—slowly, of course.

I stretched out on the sofa and put my feet in his lap. "Are you paying attention? I'm not going to show you this again."

Oh, diary, can you imagine? Dick began to massage my feet. He rubbed my soles, pulled each of my toes, ran his hands up my legs like two snakes slithering up a tree, and he pulled me toward him. We were both laughing, though I don't know why, and the strangest sparks ran up and down my legs, and it went on forever till I thought I would explode like a firecracker.

"Why don't you loosen your tie, Professor?" I said. "It's Saturday, after all." I raised one leg and ran my toes under his chin. Dick is such a stuffed shirt. I think he even combs his arm hairs. At least he had his jacket off and his sleeves rolled up so he could show them off.

I kept tickling his chin with my toes until he grabbed my foot and put it on his lap. Then he FINALLY loosened his tie.

I am so wicked. Mum would strangle me. I lay there, nipping at my peach, licking the juice off my fingers, pretending to ignore Dick, watching him watching me out of the corner of my eyes, until I finished the last bite. Then I tossed the pit at him. This time he caught it, the goon.

"So, Professor," I said. "What shall we do today?"

Dick kept rubbing my feet, pressing them into his lap. He was breathing harder, too.

"Do you believe in fate?" I asked. "Star-crossed lovers and all that?" I crossed my arms behind my head.

Poor Dick. He looked alarmed. "I don't know what you're talking about, my dear." He stopped rubbing my feet.

"Oh, don't you? Well, then I guess I'd better show you." I giggled and straddled his legs. Then I laced my fingers behind his head—oh, his hair is like velvet, so thick and soft—and KISSED HIM ON THE MOUTH. It was so quick. I had no time for the tongue and all that.

"Mary Alice, behave yourself," he said, grabbing my arms and pinning them behind my back. But he didn't fool me.

"Hey, Professor," I said, skipping over to the phonograph. "Maybe we should dance? How 'bout it, a waltz or a tango, or do you just want to jitterbug?" I began flipping through the records when the phone rang.

It was his publicist. Something about the book tour. I turned up the music.

"Would you mind?" Dick glared at me. "This is business."

"Well, of course," I said. "Of course, I'll just run along and be a good girl. Seen and not heard and all that. You spoil sport." And that was that, end of fun. End of life.

Because Mum, of course, came home, her arms piled with garment bags and boxes, and sent me off to take dumb Patty Fairchild to the movies (_Kiss of Death_ — I shall shove Mum down the stairs!).

But that wasn't the worst of it. Mum is sending me away to camp. For the whole summer. Molly will not be able to dally with her Dick. At least I'm going to be with Chrissy. Mum has talked to Chrissy's father (how she did that and spent so much dough in one afternoon, I'll never know—she bought enough gowns and shoes to open her own department store), and I am to leave tomorrow! I can't bear it.

Wednesday, June 25, 1947

It is hopeless. Mum hasn't left me alone with Dick for even an instant. And Dick seems perfectly content with her plans. He hasn't done a thing to talk her out of sending me away. The traitor.

I will show them both.

Thursday, June 26, 1947

Well, I am banished. Mum drove off with me last night, without even giving me time to say good-bye to Dick. He was not even out of bed, his door still closed.

Darling Dick, don't forget your dearest Molly!

Later: so much for devoted Dick. HE IS MARRYING MUM. The two-timer.

Mum just called. "You should see my ring, Molly, dear," she gushed. "You never saw such a gorgeous diamond—and three times as big as the one your father gave me. Naturally, we'll postpone the honeymoon until after Richard's summer courses are over. But it will be worth it— we'll have the whole year traveling around the country while Richard promotes his book and teaches. It's SOOO _romantique_. And Molly, you can go to boarding school with Chrissy." She blabbered on about how there was no need for me to come home for the wedding and miss all the fun at camp. Of course not, a daughter at the wedding would spoil the glamour and romance. To say nothing of the anguish when the groom smooched too long and enthusiastically with his new stepchild at the reception—and announced he was taking her on the road trip, too.

"I'm brimming with happiness," I said and burped. "Look, Mum, I'd love to hear all about how he popped the question, but it's time for canoeing."

How could Mum compare Dick's ring to Daddy's? And how could Dick forget me? I'll make them both sorry. They'll see how camp improves my character.

Monday, July 7, 1947

DEAR MOLLY,

Professor Richard and I are now husband and wife. He gave me the most luxurious mink coat for a wedding gift.

I have begun making arrangements for you to attend school with Chrissy. Your stepfather and I will stop by to visit you at camp before we leave for New York City, but Chrissy's father will pick you up from camp in August, as we expect to be in Chicago by then.

Mon cher mari is so devoted—he even offered to take you with us on the book tour. However, I told him under no circumstances could you neglect your studies for an entire year. Can you believe, the dear thing, he said he'd arrange for private tutoring at the universities where he'll be teaching, but I said there was no need to be so extravagant. Especially for a young girl who would scarcely appreciate the effort and expense.

Besides, my dear, you would feel quite left out, as we newlyweds will be cooing at each other like doves. You'll be much happier with Chrissy, I'm sure.

The dear man is teaching class now and quite busy with preparations for the trip, but I am sending along his love.

I thought you might like to see the enclosed. Can you believe your own mother is a blushing bride! Sometimes I have to pinch myself.

LOVE,

YOUR MOTHER

(MRS. RICHARD RICHARD)

Richard-Liddell Nuptials

Catherine Liddell and Dr. Richard Richard were joined in holy matrimony in a private service at Sage Chapel, Cornell University, yesterday.

The bride is a graduate of Charleston High School, Charleston, Illinois, and the Charleston Secretarial School.

The groom is distinguished visiting professor of literature at Cornell and author of the best-selling *Hunting in the Enchanted Forest*.

After a year-long honeymoon coinciding with the groom's book tour and teaching engagements around the country, the couple will be at home in Wellesley, Mass., where the groom is professor of literature at Wellesley College.

molly wrote nothing about her mother's letter and wedding announcement. That the article did not mention the bride's daughter must have crushed her.

My relationship with my own mother, with my grandmother, was so unlike Molly's and Mrs. Liddell's that I could not comprehend it. When I tried out for the basketball team in eighth grade, Grandma Keckler sat on the bleachers, knitting and nodding encouragement while I ran through the drills and exercises that would determine who made the JV team. When I led the varsity team to the league championship, Grandma, Mother, and Father were all at courtside, cheering. Afterward, Mother threw a party for the team, complete with a German chocolate cake decorated like a basketball.

I could not imagine her competing with me. Indeed, she spent countless afternoons with me in the darkroom, listening to my tales of triumph and tragedy as she submersed her photographs in their chemical baths.

When, at sixteen, I burst into tears because all my friends had bought chunky platform heels for the Christmas formal, Mother took me to Chicago to find an elegant pair of flats with satin laces that wound about my ankles and created an illusion of elevation without boosting me to well over six feet.

True, I still resented the genes that had cursed me with my height (for despite my success on court, I would have given anything to gaze up into Bobby Baker's eyes), but I could not fathom why Molly's mother saw her daughter as a rival and a threat. I berated myself for not telling Mother at the time about Mrs.

Liddell's fury over the scorched dress, her ransacking and destruction of Molly's wardrobe. Yet I had to admit I'd been mortified when Mother, her waist as expansive as a continent, her skirts as dowdy as a nun's, had come to visit at the hospital, especially when my doctor, who could have doubled for Gregory Peck, stopped by my room to chat.

Then, too, in comparison with Molly's life, mine seemed everything that was temperate and wholesome. I envied her her recklessness.

Friday, July 11, 1947

Diary!

I canoed through the rapids today with Chrissy! _C'est merveilleux, n'est-ce pas?_ We're the only ones in our cabin who were brave enough.

Then we practiced swamping and righting our canoe downstream, where the creek is so calm you can see the sky in it. I felt so wonderfully SLIPPERY, like an eel. And wet, wet, wet, as if I never lived on land. In school last year, we read that Hindus believe in reincarnation. Maybe I was an eel in my past life. An eel. A seal. I feel it could be real.

My ears are still full of water. It rattles inside when I shake my head.

I'm so deliciously sleepy. Good night, diary dear!

Tuesday, July 15, 1947

Chrissy taught me the most wicked words to Mum's favorite hymn! "I was sinking deep in sin. Gin lifted me!"

Chrissy says gin and tonics are the best. She tried to smuggle a bottle in her bedroll, but her dad found it. So we are high and dry. Oh, my.

Now that we can manage the rapids and portage the dam, Chrissy has promised to take me on a great adventure. But first, she says, we must somehow get some booze.

I can't wait.

Saturday, July 19, 1947

Campfire tonight. The sing-alongs were so corny.

Dick sent me a box of chocolates today. "Don't tell your mother," he wrote. As if I tell Mum anything!

I gobbled up all the chocolates after dinner. Sweets for the sweet! Molly's tummy hurts tonight. But she is ever so content.

Monday, July 21, 1947

We're going to the boys' camp down-stream this weekend.

"It's going to be a rite of passage," Chrissy says. "An initiation."

Maybe I should paint my face, the way dear Betsy and I did that night oh so long ago! I'm partial to pink stripes and yellow dots these days. (I wonder if Betsy has forgotten me. She would think me a most scandalous _jeune fille_, I suppose, if she saw me now.)

I saw the most gauzy yellow butterflies in the meadow behind the mess hall today. It made me think of dear, sweet Daddy. He could have told me what they were. I am so stupid without him. Dull, dull Molly.

An initiation is just what I need.

I have refused to answer Dick's letters.

And Mum has refused to write me since our last phone call. So we are even.

Sunday, July 27, 1947

Wait till I tell Dick what I learned at camp. He'll be so jealous. Mum tells me all the time to be more accommodating. Well, I have taken her advice. I am so tempted to send a postcard home and tell them about my escapades.

Diary, you'll never guess what we did. The river was so high—it rained all last night—and we took the canoe out today. I thought we'd drown for sure—the water came right over the bow—huge, huge waves and troughs.

When we finally reached the dock at the boys' camp (my hair was dripping and my T-shirt CLUNG to me), a boy Chrissy knows named Teddy was waiting for us along with his buddy Ronald.

They had a bottle of sloe gin and an old blanket. We hiked through the woods

molly 111

till we came to a clearing, where we spread out the blanket. I was so hungry, diary, and they had NOTHING to eat. I thought I would DIE of hunger, but the sloe gin was so ruby red, I thought if I drank enough, maybe I wouldn't be hungry anymore.

Then the boys started taking off their clothes. "Let's go skinny-dipping," Teddy said. "Last one in's a rotten egg."

Chrissy already had her blouse off. "What's the matter, Molly? Are you chicken?" she asked.

"Of course not," I said. I pulled my T-shirt over my head and hung it on a branch. Then I stepped out of my shorts and underpants. "Okay," I said, "let's go."

We followed the boys through the woods until we reached a small blue lake ringed with trees. Ronald grabbed me as soon as I jumped in and pushed me under.

"You creep," I said. I hit him in the ribs with my elbow, and he let go.

Teddy and Chrissy were making out, right there in the water. She had her legs wrapped around him and her arms around his neck.

"Hey, doll." Ronald was behind me again, whispering in my ear. He had his hands on my breasts.

"I'm not your doll," I said. "Go fly a kite."

But he turned me around and started kissing me. He's not my type, diary. He has red hair and his arms and legs are a mass of freckles, but he was a great kisser. I pretended he was Dick.

Anyway, he took my hand and put it over his you-know-what, which was sticking up out of the water like a fat pink worm.

"That's good," he said, as if I were being graded. "Damn, I wish I had a rubber." Diary, I felt so wicked. He carried me out of the water, and we went to the blanket. Chrissy and Teddy had disappeared in the woods.

"Don't worry," Ronald said. He lay down

molly 113

on top of me. "I won't stick it inside you. That way you won't get pregnant."

Diary, I scarcely cared what he did. It was such glorious fun, although the blanket was damp against my back, the ground was so wet.

I have such a headache now, and Chrissy and I are grounded for taking the canoe out in such rough water. KP duty all week and in bed before lights out. I don't care.

If Dick thinks he and Mum can leave me behind in New York while they tour the country, he's in for a surprise. I plan to be impossible to desert.

the summer Molly spent at camp, I myself first went to the beloved Ozarks of my father's childhood. The three of us spent our days hiking. I remember standing sweaty and triumphant on an outcropping of sun-warmed rock, surveying the green-furred mountains around us. Father unpacked his knapsack while Mother and I spread a blue-checked cloth on a large flat rock. We ate peanut butter and jelly sandwiches because I was scheduled to get braces when we got home, and certain foods would be off-limits. I savored the creamy, sticky peanut butter that stuck to the roof of my mouth while hawks soared on thermal currents high above.

Night after night, the images of Molly's life and mine played before my eyes. Now Molly was dead, and I might just as well be. My room smelled of menthol and stale air, my sheets of bleach and sweat. I wanted to kick off my covers and scream, but even the thought left me weak. I hated my body more than ever. I was still too tall, but now I did not even have the magic of the court to lessen my regret.

During the day, I was lethargic. I lost interest in my studies. Grandma Keckler was tutoring me in French.

"Je veux mourir," I said, remembering lessons with Molly.

Grandmother put down her book and took my hand. Hers was still strong, but blue-veined, like fine lace.

"I know how you feel," she said, "or at least somewhat."

She paused. I waited. "I had a son Noah," she continued. "Do you know why no one ever talks about him?"

The clock ticked, ticked on my nightstand. I felt as if she

were about to reveal some truth at once dreadful and illuminating.

"I found him in the barn," Grandma said, "hanging from the rafters. I cut him down myself. I never understood why he did it. The Depression had been hard on us, but we were luckier than others. We still had the farm. We had each other.

"I've never forgiven myself for failing to give him the strength and faith to carry on. I want you to have that strength and faith, Betsy. I want you to keep them inside you, where no one can take them away."

She held my hand tighter, with a tenacity at once surprising and expected. "Look at me, child," she said, taking my chin in her other hand. "Will you promise me that whatever life has in store, you will face it?"

"Yes," I said. "I promise." I wondered if I could keep that promise, if I was strong enough. But I realized that I wanted to, I had to. How could I give up, when Molly never did? Suicide was easy—you just let someone else pick up the pieces. I could not do that, not to Grandma, to my parents, not to Molly. In my damaged heart, I made a vow that I would live for all of them. But it was Molly's story, more than anything, that compelled me to keep faith. I vowed that day to write my life as if it were her love letter, a candle lit against the darkness. She would be my heart flame, and I would never let her down.

Friday, August 15, 1947

Dick arrived unannounced at camp today. Mummy has been hospitalized, but he won't say for what. We're going to see her tomorrow. Tonight we're staying at this swank resort in the Finger Lakes. Diary, it's so posh you can't even wear jeans, and they serve tea before the fire every afternoon. Dick has promised to take me horseback riding. I could swoon!

Mummy's okay, Dick says, as if I should believe him. In any case, he looked like he slept well. When he picked me up this morning, he was wearing pressed slacks and shirt, a cashmere sweater draped around his shoulders. The picture of desolation.

"You look pained, <u>Dad</u>," I said.

"Molly, this is no time for wisecracks," said my humorless stepfather. "We're already late."

"Ever hear of the phone?" I folded my arms across my chest and scratched a mosquito bite on my leg with my shoe.

Dick was dabbing at his temples with a handkerchief.

Mummy must be really sick. I can't imagine her letting me alone with her dahrling hubby. She's got to be furious I'm spending the night with him. He's downstairs in the lounge now, having a nightcap. Drowning his sorrow, no doubt. I searched his luggage for a phone number at the hospital, but he must have it in his jacket pocket. Or he memorized it instead of writing it down. He's so secretive about everything. What's up, Dick? What did the doc say, Dick? The DOC, Dick, DOC.

He had champagne with dinner, but he wouldn't let me taste it.

"A cherry Coke for the young lady," he told the waiter.

"I'm not a young lady," I said. "I can prove it, too." I reached across the table for his glass. "Here's looking at you, kid!" I said and took a sip. Won't he be jealous when he finds out about Ronald? When he

comes back, I'm going to surprise him.
I feel as if there are bubbles rising
inside me right now.

I've been mysterious about camp. In
the car, Dick kept asking me what I
did—like a detective. I didn't give him
any satisfaction. Just the usual swimming,
canoeing, arts and crafts, the sing-alongs
around the campfire.

"What about after the campfire?" he
wanted to know.

"After the campfire, we returned to
our cabins, said our prayers, and bedded
down for the night. All the fresh air and
exercise wore us out. A cabin of healthy,
tired girls," I said. I did give a hint
about Ronald. Nothing specific. Just that
I had done something naughty. He
probably thinks it's smoking, which he
despises.

"You," he said, kissing me on the forehead as if I were a child before he went
downstairs for his drink, "should be
brushing your teeth, Molly, and taking

your bath. And don't forget to wash behind your ears."

"Under my arms and between my legs, too. Right, _Dad?_ Are you going to inspect me afterward?" I am sooo wicked. He actually blushed.

"Off with you," he said, swatting my behind.

"Toot sweet!" I saluted him. He hates it when I butcher my French. It's so uncouth. Forsooth, I'm an uncouth youth!

He was watching, so I pulled off my blouse on the way to my bath, pirouetted, and blew him a kiss before I closed the door.

"Molly, your sense of modesty is appalling," he said. The stern father.

Mummy would ship me off to a convent right away. Sister Mary, Our Lady of Chastity. Yes, I'll minister to little orphan girls, give them French lessons. "_Je suis votre serviteur, monsieur. Que voulez-vous? Que je vous embrasse? Bien sûr!_"

Well, I will practice my new skills with Dick. He'll be back soon. I forgot what a hunk he is!

If Mum tries to send me off to private school after tonight, Dick will put his foot down. I know he will.

Well, diary, I have to turn off the light and lie in wait like Sleeping Beauty.

molly did seduce her stepfather. She gave no details of the seduction in her journal, but I imagine her tossing off her nightgown and panties as Ava Gardner might have discarded a boa. Molly never tanned deeply, but her skin acquired a pinkish, golden hue, as if, like a ripening peach, she had absorbed something of the sun itself.

In summer, when we took our baths together before my mother put us to bed, Molly would bat her eyes and blow soap bubbles at me from her end of the tub. We sat face-to-face, our backs and buttocks against the cold porcelain, our legs straddling each other's rosy, slippery legs. Once, Molly pressed her feet and toes against my vulva, which she kneaded unconsciously, rhythmically, as she lathered herself with soap.

I imagine his anticipation as she straddled him; perhaps he held his breath as I did then, in disbelief. No doubt, his face grew hot, and deep within him something stirred, something urgent and forbidden.

After our long-ago bath, that night under the covers, I lay quite still, knees clenched and bent almost to my chest, troubled by the wet, insistent throbbing between my legs. Molly was asleep, unaware and unconcerned. Sometimes when we climbed the basketball standards, the cool, smooth metal rubbed against our panties and produced the same sensation I felt that night, but I never connected it with the flint-against-steel friction between Bogey and Bacall.

Richard Richard knew, however—he knew. When his twelve-year-old stepdaughter draped herself across the bed,

unbound hair spilling across his lap, he knew what caused him
to take the small hand caught in the tangle of silky mane and
clasp it to his groin. When she knelt before him, explored his
mouth with her tongue as she undid the buttons of his shirt, he
knew why his breathing slowed and halted as he drank her in.
When she took his sex in her hands and pumped it gamely, he
knew why it leapt and quivered between her fingers. He knew all
this and more.

He knew everything that she did not.

Saturday, August 16, 1947

We passed by a graveyard of tree stumps today. A whole forest cut down and the poor, unwilling trees hauled away, cut and bleeding! There were piles of burning debris—what a horrible stench and miserable black clouds of smoke. Dick, the beast, stared straight ahead. What does he care about anything?

Mummy is dead. He said she died from food poisoning from eating spoiled potato salad she left out on the kitchen counter. I think he poisoned her himself.

He hurt me horribly. I thought I would burst into a million pieces.

I am bleeding. He glared when I made him stop at a drugstore and buy me sanitary napkins.

I can barely walk.

Oh, diary, what is to become of me? Do you remember when Betsy and I used to help Daddy catch butterflies? How long ago it seems. Another life.

Sunday, August 17, 1947

I asked Dick about the funeral today. "Why didn't you send for me?" I said. "I should have been there."

"I wanted to spare you, my dear Molly. You've already lost a brother and a father." He stared out the windshield through the rain. The wipers pumped back and forth like the headboard hitting the wall last night.

"Stop it," I shouted. "Stop it." I covered my ears. "You're lying."

"My melancholy Molly, don't whip yourself into a frenzy," he said. He took one hand off the steering wheel and put his arm around my shoulders.

"Don't!" I said. "Don't touch me. Leave me alone. I hate you."

He got us a room with twin beds tonight.

But then, diary, in the middle of the night, I crept into his bed.

I don't know what to do. Poor Mum was right. I should have been a boy.

m o l l y   1 2 5

Monday, August 18, 1947

Oh, diary! I can't stop thinking about Mummy. Dick has not shed one tear. All he thinks about is . . . you-know-what. I'm sure he killed her.

It is all my fault!

Oh, Mum. To think how I deceived you. How WE deceived you. The way he used to kid around with me when you weren't looking. "Isn't she ridiculous?" his eyes said. "Isn't it amusing the way she puts on airs?" his smile said. "Can you believe her awful French?" his arched eyebrows said.

And I said, "Yes, she's gauche," with laughing eyes. "Oh, yes," I said with my hips as I danced across the floor, "she is easily fooled." And "Yes," as I held his hand in secret at the movies. Oh, Mummy, I was everything you accused me of being and more. Insolent and selfish. A shameless flirt.

Well, I have paid for it, Mum, and so have you.

He says he hasn't done a thing I didn't ask for. I hate him. Diary, it is too horrid to think about, that he could do what he did knowing Mummy was dead. He moaned, diary, he moaned.

At first I felt all tingly. But then I felt as if I couldn't breathe. He was everywhere. His hands, his mouth, his . . . I wish I were a snake so I could shed my skin, crawl right out, and leave it behind. Daddy had a wonderful snakeskin, all powdery and dry, in his lab.

I did ask for it. I did. I have no one to blame but myself. I am a wicked, wicked girl.

HE (I will not say his name!) pretends that I have got my period. That I'm all grown up. That everything is swell. Normal. Healthy. "Just the thing when one is abandoned and alone." Those were his very words.

"Ah, you've become a young lady," he said when I told him I was bleeding Saturday morning.

"I have not and you know it," I said. "You're a creep."

He bought me chocolates then, and more dresses, a real ruby ring, which I refused to wear (I threw the dresses he had bought me across the room that morning. I should have thrown them out the window!), and I can't bother to tell you what else.

The weather is so dreadfully hot. I wrapped a scarf around my neck—I have a horrid bruise—and I thought I would suffocate. In the car, he kept trying to pull me over next to him. Once he tried to stop. "No," I said, "no." I blew the car horn.

"Your manners are appalling," he said once we were back on the road. "Come now, give your father a kiss."

"You're NOT my father," I shouted. "Keep your hands off me, you ape!" I moved as far away as I could, against the passenger door. I thought about shoving the door open and rolling out, like in the movies. I should have told the man at the hotel desk that morning when we checked out. He looked at me as if he knew.

The pervert (I won't call him Dad!) is taking me on his miserable book tour. To think I once said I'd do anything to go with him.

Wouldn't book lovers everywhere be shocked to learn their beloved author is nothing but a dirty old man. He puts on such airs. He plans to adopt me when the tour is over, he says. Good for a few more book sales, sans doute.

"You are my stepdaughter," he said this morning, inspecting his cuffs in the mirror. "I am responsible for your education and well-being."

"Stop drooling, you lowlife," I said. "You think you've won, but you haven't. Just wait."

Later: I tried to call Chrissy at a pay phone from the airport, but he caught me. He said if I tell anyone, it will be in the newspapers, and everyone will know what a dreadful, deceitful girl I am.

"I wouldn't want to have to expose you as the pathological liar you are, my dear. You can imagine the sympathy my readers would have for me. The beleaguered widower bearing up under his step-daughter's abuse and ingratitude. Not a pretty story, to be sure."

Tonight we are somewhere in the Rocky Mountains. But it's dark, and there's nothing to see. Dick played the doting dad at dinner and spread his overcoat across our laps. Then he took my hand and shoved it down his pants. I squeezed it hard and he let go of me. Ha! What could he do? The waitress came by and offered me another cherry coke.

Dick is so pathetic. He smiled at her and patted my hand. Ever an eye out for a fan. Well, if I'm to be his book tour mascot, he's going to have to pay.

when, at eighteen, I first read of Molly's rape, I did not think of it as such. I had no words, no definitions, to contain what had happened to her. I felt as if something hungry and formless had been loosed into the air, while Molly hovered, limned and luminous, at the vortex of desire.

I said nothing, then or later, to my parents of what the diaries contained. Every night, I saw the shadow of her stepfather, hovering over her, blotting out her essence.

That spring, Bobby Baker asked me to the senior prom. I had returned to school in April, but I tired easily. During gym class, I played jacks with Edith Harmon, who had broken her leg, on the bleachers while Nelly and the rest of the girls ran and jumped and shouted on the softball field. The air smelled green and new, but my legs ached. My muscles had atrophied from the months in bed. Sometimes when I walked, my body crumpled beneath me, and I collapsed on the ground.

Even so, Dr. Wilson agreed I could attend the prom, though I could not dance and would have to be home by eleven.

When Bobby arrived, Mother helped me pin on the corsage of pink and yellow rosebuds he had brought. I was touched; he'd remembered the color of my gown was lemon yellow. We took off in his father's Bel Air, and he drove me to the high school with exaggerated care, coming to a gentle halt at stop signs, pressing the gas pedal and releasing the clutch with slow and smooth precision. I was grateful for his attention to his driving because I found myself at a loss for anything to say. He looked so solemn in his rented tux, so unlike the boy with whom I'd sunk so many basketballs.

At school, the gym was decorated with large murals of Paris, the Eiffel Tower, the Arc de Triomphe, the Champs Elysees. We sat at a "sidewalk café" and sipped ginger ale while couples whirled about to strains of Perry Como's "Don't Let the Stars Get in Your Eyes." When the band played Percy Faith's "The Song from *Moulin Rouge* (Where Is Your Heart?)," Bobby took my hand and led me to the dance floor.

"Don't worry," he said, taking me in his arms, "I'll hold you up."

He held me close, making sure not to crush the roses blooming on my chest. He smelled of deodorant and aftershave, clean yet exotic, like oatmeal and cinnamon.

"This is nice," he said.

I did not pull away, as I had during the hayride the year before. Above us, the mirror ball revolved, so that the air seemed buoyant with fireflies and stars. Later, we stood beneath the stars on the walk outside my house, and it seemed as if we had danced the whole way home, as if that dance had never ended, as if our feet, imperceptible in motion, had floated above trees and lawns and silent streets, propelled only by the charge of Bobby's hand at my back.

"I'd like to kiss you," he said. His voice was somewhere near my ear, brushing against my hair. I closed my eyes, turned my face to his, and realized in the months I'd been an invalid, he'd grown taller than me.

Thursday, September 4, 1947

Dick and I are shacking up in yet another dump where the hot water runs out before you even get your head wet and the mattress leans like a sinking ship.

Dick apparently doesn't rate the "author's suite" at first-class hotels. I have discovered that readers of Hunting in the Enchanted Forest are generally women like Mum—the dimmer members of the Women's Club, book club, Friends of the Library. They drool over Dick, bobbing their feathered hats, offering him tea and sherry and cucumber sandwiches.

Poor Mum. I'm sure he killed her.

I myself think Dick's book is trash. A review in the paper yesterday called it "a fanciful tapestry of myth and romance, reminiscent of such lovers as Guinevere and Lancelot." Yes, and "The Phantom" is a "fanciful tapestry of myth and heroism, reminiscent of such warriors as Hercules and Thor."

molly's diary entries from August 1947 to August 1948 were erratic. Some days she wrote nothing at all. Other times she merely jotted down, "FIVE times today," or "Disgusting. While parked beside a school playground." She devoted a great deal of energy to finding private times to write and secret places to stash her journal.

On September 26, she gloated, "Ha! I've fixed the old stinker. I caught him rooting through my purse yesterday. I lifted a pack of cigarettes while he paid for gas this afternoon and crammed them in my purse. Then I threw it on the bed when we checked into our motel. He ranted on and on about how coarse it is for girls to smoke. All the while, I slipped my diary from my coat pocket, which he was sure to check next, to a hiding place beneath the rug! Mary, Mary, quite contrary!"

Over the course of the year, however, Molly wrote less and less often of her relationship with her stepfather, nor did she mention her mother anymore. She still wrote of her father—mostly envisioning her life if he had lived—but while she missed him, she no longer seemed as passionate for science.

Molly had a collection of more than two hundred postcards on which she'd scribbled dates of their visit, at least one from every state in the continental United States. Despite the horrifying circumstances of her road trip, I longed to tour the exotic landscapes, quaint towns, and crowded cities she had seen. The Golden Gate Bridge stretched blithely across San Francisco Bay, the purple-brown hills of Marin County basking in sunshine and shadow. Rows of palms lined the streets of Beverly Hills. In

Charleston, South Carolina, the pinks and yellows of grand old houses were softened by the light of that balmy, lazy latitude. Gazing at a barber-pole-striped lighthouse along the Outer Banks of North Carolina, I felt the spray from the breaking waves on my skin, the salt air rush into my invalid's lungs. I hiked beneath dripping oaks and maples in an Appalachian forest; stood awestruck before the Grand Canyon, marveling in the layers of mauve and red that reflected the setting sun. I stuck my head out the window and felt the air, humid and suffocating or cold and bracing, rushing through my hair; watched the soil change from rich, violet loam to packed, red clay to gritty, brown sand; the trees from crimson-stained maples, to tall and fragrant long-leaf pines, to sagebrush and tumbleweed, to solemn sequoias that seemed to belong to a land of giants who had long disappeared from the earth. Sentenced for what seemed forever to my bed, I longed for the weeks and months Molly crisscrossed the country. Yet she wrote nothing of the sights she'd seen.

She did keep an astounding tally of the purchases she cajoled from her stepfather, often with a gleeful notation, such as "Ha, I convinced the old goat to buy me new jeans and a black, two-piece swimsuit today. He forgot that he bought me the very same suit last week, so while he was at the men's counter getting some new shirts, I returned the suit and pocketed the dough." She bought and stained and outgrew and lost thirty-three dresses, gingham and calico, polka-dotted and shirred, smocked and puff-sleeved. She wore out or tired of sixteen pairs of jeans and twenty-five pairs of shorts—the latter in an assortment of reds, pinks, blues, greens, and yellows. She donned eleven halter tops, fourteen midriffs (navy, powder blue, and white among her favorite colors), and a record fifty-three T-shirts. She collected eleven jump ropes, two pairs of skates, high-heeled ballroom dancing sandals, a skiing ensemble— *"Très chic! Je suis adorable!"*—swim fins and mask, a ten-gallon hat, red cowgirl boots, and 124 marbles, including seventeen green cat's eyes. She traveled with a set of jacks, four lucky dice, and five packs of playing cards. She read, by her count, at least 1,001 comics and 299 movie, teen, and ladies' magazines. She bought newspapers from 278 towns. She went to the movies at least once a week and saw nine films more than four times.

She wrote little of the succession of tutors her stepfather engaged during their stopovers on the book tour. These came when they stayed for several weeks in college towns where Dr. Richard gave guest lectures and taught master classes. The tutors were all women, most unmarried, all elderly and plain. "I can scarcely distinguish Miss Perkins from Miss Jenkins," Molly wrote. "I am so dreadfully bored."

Nor was she impressed with the publicity surrounding her stepfather's book tour. "Dick is in the papers again today," she wrote. "What a yawn. When he's out, I replace all the clippings in his scrapbook with obituaries—of course he never bothers to look at the earlier pages. When he's old and languishing in some dreary rest home, I hope he brings them out to show the nurses. What a laugh! I almost wish I could be there."

Molly noted an odd assortment of personal milestones:

Number of nights when she did not cry in one month: three. ("But determined," she wrote. "Getting better and better.")

Number of pimples erupted in a week: also three.

Number of freckles on her stomach: none. On her right thigh: seven.

Record number of malted milkshakes consumed in twenty-four hours: five.

Record number of cherry Cokes in the same period: ten. ("Dreadful stomach pains," she wrote.)

Number of minutes required to consume a plate of spaghetti (using the spoon-twirling method): eleven.

Record number of minutes of successful escape from her stepfather: 147 (with the aid of two "swell guys" who ran the concession stand at an amusement park and with whom she hid out and "necked" in the fun house before riding the roller coaster five times nonstop).

Number of times in a week she "stumped the chump"—an oblique reference to some guessing game she and her stepfather played: six. "Dumbbell Dick is getting senile!" she crowed.

She recorded the date she crossed the Mason-Dixon line: October 14; the date her period began: June 16 ("Ugh, I can't go swimming! And it hasn't stopped Dick's disgusting games at all. 'That's why motels provide extra towels,' he said. The oaf."); the date Marlon Brando debuted in *A Streetcar Named Desire* on Broadway: December 3 ("Oh, I wonder if Chrissy will get to meet him! I am so envious. Never, ever, depend on the kindness of strangers.").

And August 15, 1948: "ONE-YEAR ANNIVERSARY. Wouldn't darling Dick be devastated to find that his dearest Molly has been diabolically unfaithful? Number of boys kissed in the past year: 342. Almost one a day. I am especially fond of juvenile delinquents. They give me quite a thrill. I have kissed boys who steal cars, carry guns, and burn down houses. And I will never forget the Spanish hunk with the wavy black hair who stole a pair of black, strappy platform sandals and black, over-the-elbow-length gloves like Ava Gardner wore in *The Killers* in return for a smooch (it was all my pleasure to oblige!) beneath the board-walk. The things Dick doesn't know! I feel quite smug."

Saturday, February 14, 1948

Dear diary,

Wish me Happy Birthday! I'm thirteen years old today. Dick's idea of a birthday greeting is you-know-what! I'd rather have a date with Dracula.

"Leave me alone," I said as he lumbered toward me.

"Molly, darling," said the huge, hairy beast, "this is how a man celebrates his lover. This is the greatest gift he can bestow." Then he pinned me down on the bed.

"Thanks," I said, pushing him away, "but I can do without the sentimentality, Dad. Let's not forget I'm your daughter." I tried to wriggle free, but he held me tighter and began again.

"I'm going to scream," I said. "It's my birthday, and I'm going to scream if you don't stop right now."

But of course he didn't. He told me I should be grateful, that I would never be worshiped like that by any boy my own age, that I should thank him for all he's spared me, not to mention his undying devotion.

I have begun to say the times tables to myself _en français_ or recite poetry— Emily Dickinson's "Dominion lasts until obtained—/Possession just as long!" That is my greatest victory.

Not that Dick seems to notice. Today he lounged around afterward and sang in the bath and ordered a full breakfast of eggs and bacon so that we were too late for tickets to the studio tours. Finally we are in LOS ANGELES (as if he's forgotten about HOLLYWOOD—how could he with the sign in the mountains visible from our hotel window!), and thanks to Dick, all the studio tours are sold out by the time we show up. Twentieth Century-Fox has Linda Darnell's costume from _Forever Amber_—and Cornel Wilde's rapier. _En garde, Dick, mon amour! Je vais te tuer._

When we finally went out, I ran up to

a man waiting for the bus and begged him to take me away. "That man's kidnapped me," I said, pointing to Dick. "He's a pervert."

It didn't work.

Dick, of course, hates a public scene. "Please, ignore her," he said—genteelly, with his oh-so-distingué accent (why does EVERYONE assume that a man who speaks with a British accent must be a gentleman?)—"she's prone to fits like this. I can't bear to put her away, you know. She's never been quite right since her mother died. Tragic, so sorry to disturb you." Then, calmly, he put his arm around my waist and, once we were around the corner, picked me up like a sack of flour and carried me off to the car.

"If you ever do that again, Mary Alice Liddell, I'll send you to the insane asylum. I've warned you, and don't think I won't." The long-suffering father.

Poor, doting Dick, he was actually sweating. He also despises perspiration in public. Unless it's on the dance floor, and even then he prefers a few perfumed beads of moisture to a downpour.

"You wouldn't dare," I said. "You'd end up in jail, and I'd escape and run right back here to Hollywood."

I crossed my legs and fussed with my skirt. Dick can't stand it when I do that. Honestly, diary, he is such a slave to his (rhymes with Dick). I took my mirror out of my purse and began patting my hair in place.

"Don't you ever humiliate me like that again," I said. "I'm grown up now, and I won't allow you to treat me like a child."

He took me to an elegant French restaurant to make it up, and I had a cheeseburger to spite him.

"Don't sulk, Dick," I said, slurping my Coke through my straw. "I'm a cheap date. You should be grateful. Some daughters would order the filet mignon." Then I kicked off my shoe and ran my foot up his leg. "What's the matter, Dick?" I asked. "Distracted?"

It is amazing how little self-control men have. I've observed that all you have to do is adjust your hem, or part your lips, or toss your curls, and they are quite unable to continue an intelligent conversation.

I ordered the <u>gâteau au chocolat avec des framboises</u> and ate ever so slowly, licking my fork for Dick's benefit.

Then while he was in the rest room, I arranged with the waiter, Tom, who is an actor and looks like Gregory Peck, to take me on a studio tour tomorrow. He has a day off and is preparing for auditions—for a MOVIE! He has already had a bit part in <u>The Story of GI Joe</u>—one of the soldiers in Company C, but so what? He worked with BURGESS MEREDITH! I can hardly wait. Tom said if we see anyone he knows, he'll introduce me.

"You've got what it takes," he said. "You

could be an actress. Shirley Temple and Judy Garland don't have a thing over you."

Just think. Maybe I'll meet a director who will ask me to star in his film, and I can leave Dick forever. One day I will, no matter what.

Tonight I will be his Molly Dolly. We are going to a huge bash in Beverly Hills, and Dick bought me a Christian Dior satin evening bag on Rodeo Drive for the event. I see it as a chance to polish my acting skills. Tonight a short farce, next week perhaps a comedy of errors.

In the morning, I will let Dick do whatever he likes as much as he likes, and then, while he's recovering, I shall meekly beg to go swimming in the hotel pool. Demure Mary Alice. Tom will meet me in the lobby at ten-thirty A.M. He has promised to teach me the articulation drill actors use to warm up before they go onstage or film a scene. You run through all the vowel and consonant combinations

as fast as you can out loud. A-ah. Ba-bah.
U-oi-ow-oo-ah. Bu-boi-bow-boo-bah. Tom said
it's like push-ups for your mouth. Here I
come, Hollywood.

Wednesday, June 23, 1948

The newsreel at the movies today said
Air Force pilot Chuck Yeager broke the
sound barrier in California last October.
The sonic boom sounded like the thunder
that used to roll across the fields back in
Charleston. Betsy and I used to count the
seconds between the lightning and thunder. Seven seconds equals one mile.

Yeager flew even faster than that—
662 miles per hour, the announcer said.
You could be anywhere in no time. Far
away before anyone realized you
intended to leave.

Dick pooh-poohed the whole thing. "The
way to see the world," he said, "is by boat
or by car. Just as we're doing." He said
men like Yeager are all swagger and

machismo. "Common," he sniffed. "Uneducated. What does he know of Petrarch or Poe? Why, during the war, he couldn't think of anything better to name his plane than the Glamorous Glynnis, after his wife. That says it all, I think."

"At least he's man enough to fall in love with a grown woman," I said, "instead of drooling over a thirteen-year-old girl."

Dick had nothing to say to that.

"If you like, Mary Alice," he said, "I shall be most obliged to hand you over to the psychiatrists. I am sure you will find the extracurricular activities at the sanitarium much more to your liking."

"In your wildest dreams," I said. "No wonder the plots of your novels are so ridiculous. You wouldn't know reality if you tripped over it."

When we got back to our room, he leered at me and took off his coat. "You need a lesson tonight, my dear. You've become quite vulgar and rude."

"Kiss off," I said.

But he shoved me down on the bed and, oh, diary, _je ne peux pas te dire ce qu'il me fait faire!_

"Pretend you're swilling down a chocolate shake," he said. "You do quite well at that, you little wench."

"I don't even hate you anymore," I told him afterward. "I feel nothing for you at all."

That got to him. He can't stand to hear me talk like that. He said he'd do anything to make it up to me, anything at all.

"My dear," he said, "the entire matter is in your lovely hands."

"Leave my lovely hands out of it, you lecher," I said. "I want to go home."

"And so you shall. We shall be home by fall. Your new home. How do you feel about that?" He had that disgusting, pleading look on his face. Like a dog that's been kicked.

"Not good enough, Dick," I said. I

looked down at the bedspread, picked at a loose thread. It's such fun to make him squirm. "I want voice lessons, too," I said finally.

"Then voice lessons you shall have," said gallant, groveling Stepdad.

He tried to kiss me good night.

"Yuck," I said. "Leave me alone. I want to go to sleep."

He is so pathetic. Wait till he's on his own and I'm a poster on his wall. I almost feel sorry for him.

when i first read this entry, I did not know what Molly had described. My grandmother had told me how French farmers produced *pâté de fois gras*, forcing a funnel between a goose's beak and pouring huge quantities of corn down its throat. I felt that something similar had happened to Molly.

There was a photograph bearing the next day's date in her scrapbook. She is standing beside an Indian in a feathered headdress beneath a sign that reads INN AND TRADING POST: IF IT IS MADE BY INDIANS . . . WE HAVE IT. ROOMS. GOOD FOOD. COTTAGES. A rack of postcards beckons from the shaded overhang behind her. Her arms dangle at her sides, and there is a vivid, dark bloom at her right wrist, just a smudge, but enough to account for the rigid, lifeless way she holds her fingers. A breeze has blown her curls out of her face and she squints into the sun, looks away from the camera, down at her anklets and scuffed shoes. The Indian squares his shoulders, head high, the brilliant feathers of his headdress quivering in the breeze. But he has contracted his rib cage, as if his breath is stuck in his belly, and the shirttail escaping from his waistband draws the eye away from the regal feathers and firm jaw to the shabbiness of his trousers, shiny with wear. He seems to gaze inward, as if only his shell has agreed to this picture-taking.

in july, after motoring back over the Rockies and crossing the Great Plains on the way East, Molly discovered John

Henry and Anna Botsford Comstock's *How to Know the Butterflies* in a northern Illinois gift shop. She demanded Dick purchase not only a copy of the book (which I still have—published in Ithaca in 1943—the Comstocks were, respectively, professors of entomology and nature study at Cornell!) but a net, cork-stoppered "killing" bottle, collecting box, mounting case, and insect pins.

"I have rediscovered," she wrote, "'lepidoptery.' Next, of course, I will need a microscope. How I miss Daddy's lab. To say nothing of how I miss Daddy. All those Saturdays with Daddy and Betsy, studying slides and specimens. The picnics in the country. Daddy was so funny, running after his butterflies, his tie flapping beneath his arm.

"I had forgotten about that. I've forgotten so much, diary. Betsy and I used to laugh till we cried. Poor Mummy, she was cross with all of us. How we lived to torment her. Drop spiders down her bra.

"Then, Sunday afternoons, tea with Betsy's Grandma Keckler —*et nos leçons français*—*et, enfin, notre mot de la semaine.* I had forgotten that, too.

"It was such fun, seeing who could come up with the most ridiculous sentences. 'I have an ecclesiastical passion for chocolate.' 'I find your labial contortions revolting. Please learn to sip more discreetly through your straw.'

"How indolent—Mrs. Thurmont taught us that one—I have become. Oh, Betsy, my beautiful butterfly, what has become of you? I suppose you would be thoroughly disgusted with me if you knew how badly I've turned out."

I remembered this entry as I was writing my valedictory address. (After my talk with Grandma, I was determined to graduate not only with my class but at the top of it.) I resolved, in honor of Molly, to use *indolent* in my speech: "Whatever paths we follow in the years ahead, we must not succumb to indolence. We must strive not only to reach but to surpass our potential, for it is in striving, again and again if need be, that we will know satisfaction and success."

That morning, I stood at the podium, believing and yet not believing in the promise of my words. The microphone amplified my voice, made it more resonant and assured. Yet as I gazed out at the assembled graduates and their families, I saw behind them the expanse of sky that stretched to the edge of the world, for by then I knew the world did have an edge. You could fall off. Molly had, and I had almost followed her.

How on this day—that a few short months ago I thought I might never see—I longed to bring her back to life, reverse her fate. I would be a female Holden Caulfield, standing at cliff's edge, the catcher in the rye.

After all, Molly was my first, best friend. That spring of my senior year it was she who pushed and prodded me out of my cocoon, out into the world beyond.

At the conclusion of my speech, a swarm of hands rose up out of the audience like wings, fluttering, flapping, the crescendo of applause rising on the breeze like Molly's butterflies.

𝒜 not long after Molly picked up the Comstock guide and all the trappings of the trade, she acquired her first specimens—several silver-spot fritillaries (Family Nymphalidae, *Argynnis aphrodite*) in a field of thistles and Queen Anne's lace adjacent a roadside restaurant near Columbus, Ohio. I examined her display case gingerly, holding my breath to avoid fogging the glass beneath which, in frozen flight, stood painstakingly labeled rows of tiny cornflower-blue and larger buttercup-yellow specimens, dwarfed by large brown moths with iridescent blue "eyes" on their wings.

The case itself was worn, the wood smooth and shiny, joints swollen. It emitted a faint smell of camphor. At the top left, I found the silver-spot fritillaries—scarcely an inch and a half long, umber bodies, umber brown wings splashed with black spots and stripes. On the underside, the wings were pale apricot and fawn with white eyes. Ranged along the edges were white markings that Molly compared to "a perfect set of pearly whites."

She also caught several cabbage butterflies (Family Pieridae—*Pieris rapae rapae*, the "Typical Form," and *Pieris rapae immaculata*, the "Spotless Form") in a vegetable patch hoed and watered by the owners of the Shut-Eye Motel—"somewhere in Pennsylvania," Molly wrote. "All I know is I had no 'shut-eye' at all, thanks to Dick, who found the cool night air disgustingly invigorating." She had pinned the cabbage butterflies—chalky, milk-yellow European invaders, which, according to Comstock, have devastated native species—next to the fritillaries.

Upon arrival in Massachusetts, on the front lawn of their new home, she captured a specimen of Gray Hairstreak, an almost monochromatic, slate-gray butterfly (Family Lycaenidae, *Uranotes melinus*) distinguished by the black-tipped orange "eye" resembling Halloween candy corn on each of its lower wings. She captured as well two elegant, albeit common, specimens of Family Papilionidae, the black-barred, lemon-yellow Tiger Swallowtail, *Papilio glaucus turnus*, and the yellow-spotted, blue-black Black Swallowtail, *Papilio polyxenes*.

Whenever I studied her butterflies, I imagined Molly, golden brown arm outstretched, waving her net in the air, swooping down on gossamer wings of ebony and sapphire, her own captivity forgotten in the sweep and rush of the net. I felt her indrawn breath as she held the tiny creature in the sunlight, the gold dust from its wings coating her fingers. I remembered Dr. Liddell's butterflies fluttering and flailing in his cyanide-laced bottle till their gossamer wings flapped once, twice, then stopped beating altogether.

I saw Molly, her back to her stepfather, seated before her case, piercing the small bodies with her long, steel mounting pins.

She was like her father. She could maintain a scientist's dispassionate attitude toward her specimens.

Dr. Liddell had shown us how to dissect a frog once, although I was too squeamish to participate until its belly had been slit and the leathery, formaldehyde-soaked skin pinned back in the tray. Even then, I stood at a distance, standing on tiptoe to watch as Dr. Liddell pointed to the various muscles for Molly to identify. He showed her how to slide a scalpel beneath a slender sheath, stringy and taut.

"Pectoralis," Molly said.

He nodded, handed her the scalpel, and pointed to muscle after muscle, which she separated and named, in confident, rapid staccato—rectus abdominus, caudofemoralis, pubotibialis.

Next, they examined the latex-bright arteries and veins, then at last the organs—stomach, liver, spleen, and heart.

The odor of formaldehyde blanketed the room. Molly's fingertips were shriveled as if she had soaked too long in the bath. But she bent low over the dissecting tray, biting her lip and tapping her saddle shoe against the rung of her stool.

I wondered how often Molly had thought of her father as she worked on her collection.

I wondered, too, what she might have become had she not died. Had her father not died.

I saw her as a scientist who spent summers in the field, brown-stained knees, raised welts from biting flies splattered across her arms and legs, almost camouflaged on her sunflushed skin, the red paint on her nails chipped, hair pulled back in a careless ponytail. She would have wintered in her laboratory, hunched over her specimens and books. Surely, she would have taught, like her father, for, unlike him, she could not have endured for long the solitude of the lab. She would have played pranks on her students, tripped them up with trick questions, played dumb—given them that vacant stare at which she excelled—to test their knowledge.

But she would have shared freely what she knew, exalted in their discoveries. I see her abandoning the lectern entirely, swooping up and down the aisles like a swallow, alighting here, now there, filling up the chalkboard with her looping scrawl.

There would have been excursions to a springtime swamp, the ground yielding and greasy, crayfish and minnows skittering through the oily, tea-stained water. No doubt, she would have packed picnic supplies—a wicker basket of peanut butter and jelly sandwiches, chocolate chip and oatmeal cookies, a bag of apples—as well as binoculars, metal pails, nets, and other trappings of scientific inquiry.

I wonder if she would have settled down enough to endure the tedious, poverty-filled years of school required for her doctorate. Somehow I think not. Like her butterflies, she never settled in one place for long.

I think she would have taught high school, and the classroom would have become her stage. And I know her students—boys and girls alike—would have adored her. Who could not?

In her memory, Molly's case now sits in a glass-topped coffee table in my living room. At night, when I have finished the day's chores and curl up with a cup of hot chocolate and a book, I pause now and then, and my gaze drifts to the butterflies suspended forever in mid-flight.

My Lady Lazarus, would that you could "rise with [your] red-[brown] hair/and . . . eat men like air." Your "Herr Doktor" Dick should be first on the list.

Thursday, August 19, 1948

Oh, diary, we are HOME at last. A new home, of course, but I shall go to school again and make friends. Dick can't possibly keep me all to himself now. Unless he changes his mind and locks me up like Rapunzel. In which case I will, of course, let down my auburn hair for the first handsome prince who stops beneath my window.

<u>La première chose que je ferais</u> will be to find a safe hiding place for you. I think one of the floorboards here in my room is loose enough I can pry it up and slip you beneath it. There are bookcases lining the wall on either side of the fireplace in the den that swivel on hinges to reveal hidden closets. Dick's professor friend from Wellesley, Pierre LaFleur (What a buffoon! He licks his lips when he smiles and he likes small boys — he had a red-faced, runny-nosed brat in tow when he showed us through the house. Wouldn't you know Dick would have a

pervert for a pal!), says the people who built the house used to hide bootleg liquor there during Prohibition. What delicious fun! But, of course, the bookcases are out as a hiding place—they'd be the first place Detective Dick would look. He skulks around and mopes nearby whenever I do ANYTHING with anyone else. Dancing, skating, skiing. I look over to the edge of the dance floor, the ice rink, the rope at the chairlift, and there's Dicky.

Diary, I'm going to a GIRLS' school. Dick must know that girls are even more depraved at a girls' school. But then, he's such a dope. He tried to converse with me—the way a father does with his daughter, what a hoot—while I was fixing my specimens at the dining room table tonight. He massaged my neck and pressed up against my back.

"Beat it, toots," I said. I didn't even look up. Poor Dick, he is so demoralized when I ignore him, which is basically all the time.

"Don't you have a kind word for your dear old father?" he whined.

"Leave me alone, Dick," I said again. "Can't you see I'm concentrating?" My dear father would have been able to help me with my beautiful butterflies. Dick wouldn't know a Nymph from a Swallowtail.

"You might tell me where you found those lovely little papillons. The brown ones, there." He leaned over to point to two of my pretty gray-brown *Cissia eurytus*, with their glittering, yellow-ringed eyes, running his hand down over my shoulder.

"Lay off, mister," I said. "And remove your hand NOW." I jabbed at him with my elbow, still refusing to look up. "For your information, they are little wood-satyrs, a great deal more appealing than SOME satyrs I know. And I found them in a thicket at the end of the street when I was copulating in the woods with the boy we met at the grocery store."

"My dearest Molly, your attempts at humor are not at all amusing," said sad-sack Dad, hulking and sulking, his two favorite pastimes after you-know-what. "You are an ungrateful girl. Obviously, I have spoiled you far too much." Hovering once again.

"You're blocking my light, Dick," I said, head still down. "Scram, would you?"

I refused to say another word and finally, sighing mournfully, he lumbered out to the living room and lowered himself noisily into an armchair and took up his writing tablet with great fanfare. Some author. You'd think he'd have his nose in his work all the time instead of sniffing around me.

Sunday, October 3, 1948

Dick is such a pathetic goat. His urges have become a swell source of money. Here's the lowdown on my new racket:

Tremper son biscuit, une fois par jour	$ .50	(par semaine)
Des seconds (dans le même jour)	.25	
Me faire des papouilles	1.00	
Faire le pompier	3.00	
Le soixante-neuf	5.00	
Des extras	2.00	

At this rate, I should be able to earn anywhere from $30 to $45 a week! Of course, when I'm out, the scoundrel searches my room—drawers, closets, beneath the mattress, behind the mirror. I'll fix him. Vivian (Bloom—my new best friend!) says I can stash my loot at her house.

Viv is such a doll. Dick loathes her, which of course makes me adore her all the more. For one thing, she's already fourteen and a knockout. Voluptuous figure. Dick likes them flat-chested and boy-legged. The other day, when he was feeling me up, he looked so pouty.

"What's the matter, Dick?" I said.

"Don't you like my new maracas?" I was sitting on his lap, naked, and I shook my chest and laughed like a hyena, which ruined his mood so completely that he gave it up. I paid for it later, but who cares!

My breasts are nothing compared to Viv's. She looks like a movie star—coal-black hair and eyes, like Cleopatra, that she lines with black pencil. Curvy hips. Great gams.

We played hooky Friday—Dick will be called into school again, of course, by Head-mistress Hays to determine whether there are problems at home—<u>Chez nous? Vous rigolez, Madame Hays, non?</u>—and caught the bus into Boston. What luscious fun! We went to this swank store and tried on formals for the Christmas dance at Dexter (the BOYS! school). Viv picked out a black satin dress that looked as if she'd been poured into it. Ray (Jones—her glamorous but good-for-nothing beau) will go wild.

She should dump him. She could have

anyone she wants. Someone who treats her right.

I found a simply fabulous shimmery gold gown, like my butterflies. I would have bought it, too, plunked down the dough right then and there, but then Dick would realize he hasn't uncovered all my hiding places. So I put down a deposit and asked the salesgirl to hold it for me. I cajoled Dick into buying it for me yesterday—I had to play *la fille avec les cuisses légères naturellement—il a toujours le démon du midi. Come, Dickie boy, viens à ta dulcinée! Et ensuite, mon salaud, casques du fric! La chose la plus belle du monde, c'est de te rouler!*

Sunday, October 31, 1948

Happy, Happy Halloween! Oh, diary, I have had such a super day. Viv and Ray and Craig Kostakovich and I went trick-or-treating tonight.

molly   1 6 3

I have been gorging on chocolate all evening!

Dick, naturally, nixed the idea last week. No unchaperoned dates, the number one rule of the Richard residence. Translation: Some nasty boy *pourrait tripoter ou, pire que ça, tomber sa petite et pure Molly. Méchante fille!* I simply climbed out the kitchen window and pedaled off—on Craig's bike, which he had stashed in the bushes—to Viv's, where I'd dropped off my costume on Friday. I was a dutiful daughter. I left Dick a note and a set of wax vampire teeth (which you can chew like gum) on the kitchen table.

I am not, of course, in love with Craig Kostakovich, or Jeremy Morrison, or Alex Frampton, or any of the boys. I'm getting quite a reputation, in fact, for my chastity and purity. Saint Mary. But I do love to hang out with the boys for Dick's sake. I get such a kick out of making him jealous. Which is not at all hard to do. I always let one of them

carry my books home from school and I
stand outside the house and talk for at
least fifteen minutes. Dick, I know, will
be watching from the upstairs window, so
I look as if I'm in absolute raptures, as
if every joke is the funniest thing I've
ever heard.

Diary dear, tonight was such a blast. I
dressed up as a gypsy—long red nails,
red lipstick, tons of eye shadow, a red
scarf tied across my head. I borrowed
Viv's costume jewelry and piled bangles
and bracelets on my arms, beaded
necklaces around my neck. I wore one of
my black wool school skirts—the one that
falls to mid-calf—but I topped it with
one of Viv's dad's white shirts and his
jean jacket. Viv was a witch—all in black,
pointed cap, broom. The boys were pirates.

We hitched a ride into Cambridge,
where nobody'd know us, and behaved like
delinquents. _Mais oui!_ We threw corn at
the houses that only gave us apples and
soaped their car windows. Then when we

got back to Wellesley, we draped toilet paper over all the trees at MY house. It was SO hard to be quiet. Dick was positively purple when I went inside—en costume, bien sûr!

He hadn't touched the teeth I so thoughtfully picked up for him. He had not eaten dinner. He had had four gins. He had driven all over town. Solicitous, salivating stepdad. Who had molested his delicious, darling Molly? He stripped the clothes right off me, right in the living room, and actually put me over his knee.

"Shall we add a little sadism to our routine?" I asked. I was laughing so hard, tears poured down my cheeks. I rolled off his lap onto the floor and held my stomach. I couldn't stop laughing. I thought my appendix might burst. It hurt so much—don't EVER eat eleven bars of chocolate and laugh like that.

"Get up, Mary Alice," said stern, disappointed Dick. His Molly is no angel.

"Get up and go upstairs. I expect you to be in bed when I get there."

I stole into the kitchen, swallowed a glass of milk (to wash down all the chocolate), grabbed the teeth off the table, popped them in my mouth, skipped upstairs to bed, and waited for dear, doting Dad. When he came into my room, I flashed him and grinned like an idiot. Exasperating brat, I am!

Wednesday, November 3, 1948

School is such a dreadful bore. Miss Crystal, the French teacher, has reprimanded me again for using "appalling filth" in class.

J'ai dit, "Je suis une petite merdeuse, n'est-ce pas?"

C'était vachement drôle! Chrissy, I am eternally grateful for your summers on the Riviera.

Miss Wade, my math teacher, swings

her hips so dangerously when she walks down the aisles between our desks that she knocks our books to the floor. Of course, we stack them at the edges on purpose and laugh uproariously when they fall.

And Miss Sims, the history teacher, is a lush. She keeps a thermos of coffee on her desk and drinks at least two cups a class. We figured there was something fishy when she tripped over her chair leg and, clinging to the lectern, peered at us over the top of her eyeglasses and said, "Now, class, what mamous fan rallied the Union soldiers at the Battle of Gettysburg?"

Last week, Viv and I sneaked into her classroom over lunch break and found a bottle of liquor in her desk. We emptied it out and replaced it with vinegar. It was a frightfully close shave. After we poured the whiskey out the window, we couldn't get it closed again.

"Slam it," Viv said.

So I did, and it made a HUGE bang.

Of course, just our luck, Fraulein Hays
was prowling the hallways. She has
nothing better to do, the old sow. She
waddled into the room, hands on her
hips, her head swiveling back and forth
like a searchlight.

Fortunately, she not only would never
make the track team, but she's also half-
blind. We ducked behind old Sims's desk
just in time and held our breath. My
heart was beating so hard. What a riot!
Diary, you should have seen Sims's face
when she took a swig that afternoon. She
choked and spluttered and ran out of the
room with her hand over her mouth. Of
course, she didn't dare accuse any of us
because then she'd have to own up to swilling alcohol in school.

We are underground heroines.

Franchement, diary, I scarcely have
time for studies. Anna Bell and I go to
the Brookline Country Club every Saturday
for ballroom dancing—I just ADORE the
club. The maître d'hôtel is such a sweet

man. He brings us Cherry Cokes when the band stops playing. I told him I'm going to be in the movies one day—that's why I'm learning to dance.

"I don't know where you young ladies find your energy," he said last week. "I have a granddaughter who's just three years older than you. She's going to be a writer—Sylvia Plath—remember that name. She's going to be famous one day."

"So am I," I said. "Remember my name, too—Molly Liddell."

I have so much to learn if I'm going to be an actress. Evelyn Ross and I take tap and ballet at Miss Jeanne's School of Dance on Thursdays—Ev is such a fireball, you should see her cut up the rug Saturday nights at Viv's—and on Tuesdays, I am taking voice lessons.

Remember when I used to torture poor Mum by banging out "Heart and Soul" and "Chopsticks" on the piano instead of practicing my scales? Now I am a devoted student of music. I run through all my vocal drills and exercises with nauseating regularity. It takes up quite a lot of time in the evenings. Time when I must not be interrupted FOR ANY REASON. Plus, the exercises are so thoroughly annoying. I sing as loudly as possible, over and over and over.

Saturday nights at Viv's are such a blast. Dear Dad has no idea what goes on. Viv's parents are always out—and EVERYBODY knows it—they have season tickets to the opera, ballet, symphony, and who knows what else? The whole gang comes over, and we have such a blast. Viv has her own jukebox with all the latest hits: Sammy Kaye's "You" and "Walkin' to Missouri." "Sleepless" and "Here in My Heart" by Tony Bennett. "Forgive Me" by Peggy Lee. Perry Como, Eddy Arnold, Russ Morgan, and—Old Blue Eyes. Plus great dance numbers like "Mairzy Doats" and "Rum and Coca Cola"—which is what we drink. Ray got drunk last weekend and started roughhousing Viv because he saw her at the movies Friday night with a Marine. What he doesn't know is that Viv had a fling with the guy last summer.

"You don't own her," I said. I don't like the way he treats her when he drinks. "It's a free country. She can go to the movies with whoever she wants."

"Stay out of it, doll face. It's none of your beeswax," he said and shoved me. He grabbed Viv by her hair and tried to force her down the hall into her parents' bedroom. I stuck out my leg and tripped him, and the other guys yanked him up off the floor and marched him outside. We watched through the window. He doubled over, vomited on the lawn, and staggered off down the sidewalk. I wish Viv would stop playing around with him. It could have been an awful scene.

Viv takes such terrible risks sometimes. She tried to kill herself when she was eleven. Her uncle raped her at his own wedding. She was a bridesmaid. He gave her champagne at the reception and then offered to take her up to her hotel room when she felt dizzy. He told her if she made a sound, he'd strangle her. And that if she told her mother, he'd say she was a liar, that he'd caught her with a bellboy when he went up to check on her.

"Maid no more," said Viv. "No white wedding for me."

Poor, dark Vivian Bloom. Her mother invites the uncle and his wife to their house every year at Christmas, and he always pulls her under the mistletoe.

We told each other our life stories one night after the gang left. We polished off the rum—Viv makes divine daiquiris!—and played Truth or Dare. That's when we discovered that neither of us is a virgin. Viv thinks it's hysterically funny that Dick still confesses his undying love to me.

"Undying lust," she said, handing me a cigarette. "Here, suck on this," she said. "I'll bet it tastes a lot better than what you get at home." I told her I go through GALLONS of mouthwash.

When Viv's parents go to Providence weekends, sometimes she hangs out at the convention hotels in Downtown and picks up men. She gets them to take her to the theater, and afterward they take her up to their rooms and do it with her. One guy gave her a hundred bucks, and another one bought her emerald earrings. She wants to know if I want to come along next time, but I couldn't stick it. Men are so numbingly dull.

I've tried to get her to stop. I've tried to get her to ditch Ray. She's too good for all of them.

the summer before I left for the University of Chicago, I devoured everything I could about college. I was terrified of leaving home. My promise to Molly that spring seemed foolish now, and futile. She had flown far, far away, and I was left behind, alone. I began to doubt again that she had ever been real.

One afternoon on my lunch break, I picked up *Mademoiselle*'s college edition at the newsstand near my father's office. He was out, so when I returned with my lunch, I kicked off my pumps, settled into his vast leather chair, and opened the magazine. I had caught up on my filing, and I needed a distraction.

I was startled when I saw Sylvia Plath listed as guest managing editor of the August issue, with the magazine's "last word on college, '53." She had become famous, after all, just as her grandfather had said.

I turned to page 358, where *Mademoiselle* had published Sylvia's villanelle, "Mad Girl's Love Song." I hoped her poem might bring Molly back, but instead it only intensified my feelings of loss and hopelessness. Sylvia wrote of mythical thunderbirds and dancing stars, of God's fall from heaven and the end of Satan's reign in hell. Her poem spoke to my own mad childhood intoxication, extinguished by the abrupt, sobering arrival of nothingness. I felt as Sylvia did: "I shut my eyes and all the world drops dead; / (I think I made you up inside my head.)."

I did not know for whom she had written it, but I knew how she felt. College loomed closer, and Molly seemed farther away than ever.

Monday, November 15, 1948

Horrible Hays called me into her office again last week. I repeat, word for word, the lecture (What a riot! I sat legs crossed, swinging my foot up and down, arms crossed, staring out the window. Perhaps I can convince Rita Hayworth to be my guardian when I move to Hollywood. After all, Mum looked just like her. Hays droned on):

"Your teachers find your behavior most appalling, Mary Alice," tapping on a report in her hand. "You blow bubble gum in French class. Apply lipstick in history. And in math, you have not completed the assigned homework for three weeks. THREE WEEKS. Moreover, you signed your name to your last test without even attempting a single problem. A single problem, let me repeat.

"Mary Alice, this is nothing to smirk about. Your IQ is well above average. You are clearly quite bright, but you show no interest or effort in a single class

outside of music and drama, where Miss
Smith tells me you delivered a passionate
speech of Ophelia's without one mistake. Yet
in your other classes—frankly, your
teachers are at the end of their ropes.

"Mary Alice, please look at me, not
out the window. I must ask you once
again, are there problems at home? Your
mother is dead. You have lied about her
death, that we know. She was not, as you
let on at the beginning of the school
year, run over by a stolen car driven by
an escaped convict. She died of food
poisoning after eating her own spoiled
potato salad. Tragic enough in itself, but
when coupled with the earlier deaths of
your father and brother—well, I am not
at all surprised that you have invented
stories about her. I confess Dr. Richard
told me about your tendency to lie, to
make up a life more agreeable to you.
Poor dear, don't think I am not
sympathetic.

"However—Mary Alice, you must FACE

FACTS, even when they are unpleasant. You cannot live in a fantasy world. Your stepfather, and forgive me if I seem blunt—circumstances warrant frankness— your stepfather is a gentleman and a scholar, but I am not entirely convinced he is knowledgeable in the matter of raising young girls, particularly those in the process of becoming young women. I suspect he may be too caught up in the rigors of university life, too concerned with writing his books and giving readings and granting interviews. Leaving you to fend for yourself far too often. Not at all what we at Dana Hall encourage. You must have a role model and a confidante.

"Mary Alice!" smacking the report down on her desk and clapping her hands. "Please, attention front and center. I must ask, as I said, whether he is aware that young girls—young WOMEN—must look to their beloved fathers for guidance on how to meet and interact with young men of their own age. You will one day, naturally, want a husband and children. That does not happen by waving a wand."

("Depends on the wand, Fraulein," I longed to say. I had the most horrible scare this month. Dick refuses to wear rubbers, and my period was three weeks late. Viv took me to a doctor in Boston. What a panic. I wore Mum's old wedding band, signed in as "Mrs. Catherine Richard," and listed my age as eighteen. Now I'm the proud owner of a diaphragm. Of course, even this, spontaneous Dick finds a hardship. I think he'd like to see me knocked up, if it weren't for the fact he'd finally get caught in the act. But let us return to Fraulein Hays.)

"Mary Alice, your father takes you out of school every time he goes out of town to give a reading. You missed an entire year of school touring the country with him last year. We at Dana Hall must keep a sharp lookout for the welfare of our young women, to ensure their adjustment in a frightfully complex world. Now, let me continue. You simply cannot miss any more classes this year. He must realize that you cannot accompany him on all of his literary jaunts. He must realize that you need to participate in activities of your own. That you require more opportunities to interact with others of your age.

"Mary Alice, without sufficient freedom to pursue your natural urges—let me rephrase—your natural ATTRACTION to young men—your ability to attend to your studies will be severely hampered. As we have already seen. We have, in fact, concluded that an unsatisfactory home situation—to be exact, your father's un-reasonable expectations, combined with his disregard for your needs—is interfering with your ability to form age-appropriate friendships with the opposite sex, which, in turn, is hindering your development—both emotional and intellectual. We graduate

well-rounded young women here, Miss
Liddell, well-rounded young women, and
we look forward to counting you among
them.

"Well, do you have anything at all to
say for yourself? Please sit up straight
and put your feet squarely on the floor."
Here she folded her hands on her desk
and waited for me to respond.

Oh, diary, it was all I could do to
keep from laughing in her face. Fraulein
Hays is SO melodramatic. And so fierce.

I told her that as far as I was
concerned, I would give my classes
exactly the attention I felt they were
worth, but that if she wished to consult
with my DAD, it was fine with me.

Friday, December 10, 1948
Diary, I have absolutely forgiven Horrible Hays. She has ORDERED—can you
imagine?—ORDERED Dick to let me
star in the spring play. She called him

into school again yesterday. He is furious with me. Says I must stop playing the fool in school.

But of course there was a price. "_Chère, Mary Alice, ma petite mignon, cette pièce va te coûter très cher_," said benevolent Dad. He took me to Evelyn's ballet recital, and as we sat in the darkened auditorium, he folded his raincoat over his lap, grabbed my hand, and put it beneath his coat. _Toujours_ the old-world gentleman.

Mais, ce n'est rien. Rien du tout.

The play's the thing.

I am positively delirious. You'll never guess what we're performing. _A Mid-summer Dream's Knight_. By William Tennessee! Viv will be Sir Lancelot, _et moi_—Lady Guinevere. Charlton Heston and Ava Gardner, move over for Viv and Molly. (Chuck and Ava played the leads last summer on Broadway, diary!)

The script is such a hoot. It's all about what would have happened if Lance and

Gwen had run away from Camelot. They have no squires or ladies-in-waiting, no cooks, no one to tend the fire or stir the soup. And no money. They give up everything—their lands and titles— EVERYTHING—to be together. So much for all that romantic slosh about undying love. She can't cook or clean. And the Knight of the cart turns out to be useless at anything other than jousting and downing goblets of wine. (Speaking of which, Dick spends almost all his evenings now getting sloshed with The Flower. He calls the play "a travesty." "A travesty," I said, "at least it's not a mockery of literature like your book!")

Here's the basic plot: Lance and Gwen escape to France (where Lance was born), trade her crown for a flock of sheep and a shepherd's hut, and make a stab at _la vie rustique._ Lance, in a drunken stupor, accidentally drives the sheep into the river, where (after singing like a Greek chorus) they drown. In the second act, they (Lance and Gwen, not the sheep) run off to London to look for more suitable work. However, now they find themselves mysteriously in the sixteenth century, the streets swarming with plague victims, living and dead. In desperation, Gwen takes a job as a barmaid in a down-and-out pub (where the ruffians make fun of her fine speech and pinch her bottom). Lance takes to the highways and byways, robbing nobility and hoarding their swords and scabbards, jeweled bracelets and baubles, to sell to lords and ladies in surrounding manors. (Once, he mistakenly tries to sell an emerald brooch back to the baroness he stole it from and barely escapes with his life.)

Finally, in Act Three, the tarnished lovers, now in the Industrial Age, lose all trace of their good looks and noble speech. Gwen turns to a life of prostitution to feed and clothe herself. (You see, diary, I am perfect for the part!) And Lance, who has abandoned her entirely, hooks up with a gang of petty thieves and pick-pockets who turn out to be the former Knights of the Round Table.

Near the end of the play, Lance shows up at Gwen's flat. He doesn't know who she is—he's only there _pour se faire sauter_. But she recognizes him, kicks him out, and joins the All Saints' Sisterhood. In the last scene, she assists at the baptism of a twelve-year-old prostitute whom she has instructed in the joys of celibacy and promise of the afterlife.

You may wonder, diary, why Dana Hall, which believes in preparing women for the Three C's of marriage—cooking, cleaning, and copulating—would perform this play, but Fraulein Hays is simply enamored of Tennessee. _D'ailleurs_, the moral lesson, as she sees it (as she sees EVERYTHING), is that a progressive approach of "sanctioned" dating and petting—reserving "going all the way" for the honeymoon—is the best insurance against the type of "fall" that Gwen experiences.

Said Hays the afternoon we read through the play, "You see, Mary Alice, why I am so eager for you to spend more time with boys your own age and less in the company of your father. It is the sheltered young woman who is most likely to take a wrong turn. It is all well and good for your father to value your virginity, but he does you no service by protecting you from the realities of boy meets girl. I do hope this play teaches you something more than dramatics."

Quick, get me to a nunnery!

Monday, February 14, 1949

Diary, I'm FOURTEEN! My Birthday Resolutions are:

1. Become an actress.
2. Escape from Dick.
3. Escape from Dick.

4. Escape from Dick.
5. Oh, did I mention, escape from Dick?
6. Become an actress.
7. Become an actress.
8. Become an actress.
9. Become an actress.
10. Become an actress.

A well-rounded list, n'est-ce pas? At Dana Hall, don't forget, we believe in being well-rounded.

Speaking of which, I have taken Fraulein Hays's advice and French-kissed Craig, Jeremy, Alex—every boy I know but Ray. (Ugh! Viv still hasn't dropped him. I keep working on her.) We played spin the bottle at Viv's last night and drank ever so much vodka. I have a dreadful headache.

Oh, diary, dear sweet Craig is such a drip. I could almost fall in love with him. At midnight he grabbed me and kissed me for what seemed like forever. Then he took my hand and led me over to the stairs. We sat down, and he held my hand and asked me to go steady.

"I'm not a virgin," I said. "You want a virgin, don't you?"

He squeezed my hand tighter. "You're such a kidder," he said. "That's what I adore about you."

"I'm not kidding. I shack up with Dick, didn't you know that?"

"Come on," he said. "Everybody knows you won't do it with any of the boys. You're not like Viv."

"Watch what you say about Viv," I said. "She's my best friend." I turned my face to the wall.

He put his hand under my chin and turned my face toward his. Diary, he was so absurdly serious. "I'm sorry," he said. "I wouldn't hurt you for the world. Won't you make me the happiest guy in the world and be my girl?"

Oh, diary, it was all I could do not to laugh in his face, the goon.

Valentine's Day/Birthday Resolutions:

1. Become an actress.
2. Escape from Dick.

(Oh, by the way, Dick gave me a pearl necklace. I shall wear it when I receive my first Oscar!)

Monday, March 21, 1949

Oh, diary, Viv and I are having such fun rehearsing for the play. We spent the weekend drinking rum and reciting our lines at her house. I am out of the house almost every night of the week. I am deliriously happy.

We've begun working on the set as well. We are building a farmer's hut with a real thatched roof—cutaway, so you can see the inside and outside at the same time. There is a stone fireplace for cooking, an old spinning wheel in the corner, and a straw-filled mattress on the floor. If only Rumpelstiltskin would teach me how to spin straw into gold!

Then, outside the hut is a babbling brook (a chorus waves long bolts of blue fabric up and down) that runs to the lake where the sheep drown (offstage—you can hear the splash). We're also painting a mural on fabric for the flat where Lance accosts Gwen and another for St. Mary Magdalene's house of mercy. The stage director will raise these up and down on a track in between scenes.

My costumes are such a scream. At the beginning of the play, I have my queenly robes and veils. Then I discard these for a peasant blouse (I get to wear a bra stuffed with falsies—I am positively SPILLING out of it!) and skirt. Then in the last scene, of course, I am wearing the somber habit of a nun. I feel like a scarecrow, floating around in heavy, black wool. It's so hot under the lights. When we wear our stage makeup, I am afraid I will melt all over my costume.

I have learned how never to upstage another actor, how to block out a scene,

how to say my lines on my mark. We are
using tape on the floor for practice, but
of course we'll memorize our movements as
well as our lines for the performance.

I have forbidden Dick to attend
rehearsals. I don't need him mooning
around like a lost dog. He has become
unbearably droopy, but I pretend that he
has shrunk to the size of an ant. I can't
even be bothered to squash him beneath my
feet. But enough.

Diary, I have saved the best for last.
In May, the week before we open,
WILLIAM TENNESSEE is coming to
direct our rehearsals. Maybe he'll take
me to Broadway or Hollywood!

Miss Smith says I light up the stage.
"You have a natural talent," she said.

I've been reading all about Tennessee
so he won't think I'm a moron when he
comes to see the play. He's a satirist, which
any fruitcake can see from the script.
And he is very big on existentialism,
which as far as I can see comes down to

Hamlet, "To be, or not to be. That is the question." To be, of course. Always to be. I dream, therefore I am.

I am thinking of writing my own play, <u>Life with Dick: Love's Luster Lost</u>. All about a girl who lost her virginity and never bothered to try and find it.

Friday, March 25, 1949

Diary, do you believe in fate? I have discovered the most incredible coincidence. Miss Smith took Viv and me to track down props and costumes for the play. A whole day without classes!

We had the most delicious time. We went to the Radcliffe Drama Department, and the director was the most glamorous woman—Hungarian, pale blond hair, long, long legs, and the most extravagant gestures. (I have been studying gestures— an actress has to have a vast repertoire. Mimi Krestovsky FLINGS her arms into the air when she speaks, as if she were a ballroom dancer.)

She never used a single first-person pronoun the entire time. It was "Mimi is so glad to meet you! Of course Mimi can help! Darlings, do call Mimi Mimi. In class, of course, you would call Mimi Mrs. Krestovsky, but here, we are all actresses together, and you must call Mimi Mimi. You have made Mimi's day. Mimi likes nothing better than helping out her young friends in the theater. Perhaps one day you will study with Mimi. Mimi has the most glorious costumes for you, and a crown, oh, yes, Mimi would be simply delighted to loan them to you."

Afterward I begged Miss Smith to visit the Museum of Comparative Zoology at Harvard to see the butterfly collection there. I am simply mad to learn more about the Gossamer-Winged family, which I have been studying in Comstock. I should so like to find an Acadian Hair-

molly 193

streak this summer. _Thecla acadica._
Rather like the Gray I found last year,
but softer brown and without the distinct
orange eye spots—just a glimmer of pale
orange on the top, but more marked on
the underside. Well, wouldn't you know,
one of Harvard's former scientists, Dr.
Vladimir Nabokov, has a divine collection
at the museum. Simply tons of Lycaenidae
specimens.

I asked the curator if I might write
to Dr. Nabokov, and CAN YOU BELIEVE
IT? He lives in Ithaca in OUR OLD
HOUSE and teaches at Cornell now! So I
am sending him a letter tomorrow to ask
where I should hunt for more specimens.
Oh, I feel quite certain this is an omen.
I biked down the street and mailed the
letter tonight.

Friday, April 1, 1949
Dick is such an April Fool. I begged
him to take me out to hunt butterflies

after school today. We drove out to Paintshop Pond, and Dick insisted that before I could chase my beloved butterflies, I had to neck with him in the backseat. He is nothing but an overgrown schoolboy. Honestly. Well, meek little Molly did her duty, then slipped away, skipping. I found three Spring Azures! They are such a lovely, pale blue. Dear <u>Cyaniris ladon lucia</u>! I lay on my back by the pond and breathed in the spring. For the stage, you must breathe deeply from the abdomen so your voice projects. I do love breathing. The air was so clean and brimming with anticipation.

When I got back to the car, Guess Who had fallen asleep in the backseat? The car was sitting on a little hill, facing the water. I opened the driver's door ever so quietly—devious Molly—put the stick shift in neutral, and released the brake. Then I went around to the back and nudged the bumper. Splish-splash. Damp and dreary Dick.

When we got home—we had to walk
back to town and call a tow truck—
dearest Dad threatened to yank me out
of the school play. But his darling
daughter reminded him that Fraulein
Hays would not be happy to learn of
certain rituals and pastimes in the
Richard household. Oh, no, she would not
be pleased. I left the poor devil sulking
on the sofa and biked off to Viv's to
practice our lines.

Dear Miss Liddell,

I am delighted to learn of your passion for butterflies. You express particular interest in the Lycaeides, the "scudderi-melissa" group. Unfortunately, I was seriously ill in my last weeks at Harvard and therefore unable to conclude my lepidopterological affairs there. Hence, many of my specimens are still packed in a chest in the MCZ laboratory.

However, I must tell you that if you are serious in your pursuit of the Lycaeides, indeed of any butterflies whatsoever, you must Go West. The environs of Boston, for that matter all of New England, are quite dismal—as is almost the entire East Coast. There are a few rare species in the Eastern states, but they are decidedly local and their appearance unpredictable.

I suggest you consider a trip to the Rockies, particularly the regions of southern Colorado and Arizona. You may be interested to know that I discovered and named a delightful midsize butterfly which I found along Bright Angel Trail in the Grand Canyon. My wife, son, and I also spent a splendid summer in Utah at the Alta Lodge, about an hour's drive from Salt Lake City in the Wasatch Mountains. (I enclose the address on a separate sheet.) There among the lupines, with firs lining the banks of the Little Cottonwood River, my son Dmitri and I rediscovered a subspecies of the Lycaeides, the melissa annetta. The scenery is breathtaking, as you might *imagine, but be prepared for strenuous hiking at altitudes between eight thousand and eleven thousand feet. Also, be forewarned that the gadflies are numerous and bloodthirsty. Long pants and sturdy shoes will spare you the agonies I suffered in tennis shoes and shorts.*

What a coincidence that my wife Vera and I have rented your former home. I must say that we find it quite drafty and have resorted to stuffing the keyholes with cotton to keep the cold at bay. I confess, as well, that with my son away at school in New Hampshire, the house is a bit large and rambling for the two of us, but I shall imagine it filled with your specimens and nets and bottles and it will seem less lonely.

Happy hunting. Write me if you have any success.

BEST REGARDS,
VLADIMIR NABOKOV

Sunday, May 1, 1949

Happy May Day! Viv and Ray (yuck) and Craig and I packed a picnic lunch and spent the day at the park. We decorated the tetherball pole with pink, blue, yellow, and green streamers and danced a May Pole Dance, winding in and out, over and under, till we were deliciously dizzy and collapsed in a heap. <u>Bien sûr</u>, the bottle of Bordeaux Viv brought along contributed to the overall sense of abandon and merriment. A loaf of bread, a jug of wine, and thou. Viv and Ray disappeared into the woods in proper pagan fashion. Craig and I finished off the wine, and the day was so wonderfully warm, I pulled him down on top of me and wrapped my legs around him. I'm positive he's never done it. He's dreadfully shy. I had such tremendous fun seducing him. Not that he let me get very far. He said it "wasn't right." That he "respected me too much."

"I'd like you to be my girl," he said.

"Craig," I said, taking his hand and holding it in my lap. "I can't be your girl."

"Why not?" he asked. He took my hand and pressed it to his lips. He is sooo gallant. I almost wished I were the virginal girl he thinks I am.

"It's too late," I lied. "I've got a beau in Hollywood. We're secretly engaged. He's waiting for me to graduate before he marries me."

Dear Craig looked thoroughly rejected and dejected. "I've never met a girl like you," he said.

"Listen," I said and patted his hand, "if I ever break it off, you'll be the first to know."

Viv thought the whole thing was a stitch.

"You're doomed, Molly," she said after we said good-bye to the boys and biked back to her house. "Craig won't ever leave you alone now. Poor dear, if he only knew the truth."

I got home inexcusably late and went straight upstairs without so much as a glance at Dick, who hunched like a huge, hairy spider down the hall behind me.

William Tennessee arrives this week!

$\mathscr{A}$ the week before I left for college, Bobby Baker asked me to go steady. We were sitting on the front porch swing, the only sounds the slap of our feet against the floorboards and a determined cricket chirping somewhere beneath the porch.

"Here," he said. "I thought you might be getting cold." He put his letter jacket around my shoulders.

"I'm not cold," I said. "I'm not cold at all." The jacket felt large and heavy on my shoulders. Bobby was leaving for West Point the next day.

"Perhaps you'd like to keep it anyway." He put his arm around me. "Something to remember me."

"I won't forget you," I said. I did feel cold, but somewhere deep inside. The night was warm. "You should keep your jacket. You might meet someone else."

"I won't," he said. "I won't." His voice was thick, insistent.

I wondered if I loved him. Since the prom, we had been what Nelly called "an item." During the summer, Bobby worked behind the counter at Wolff's Drug Store, and every day at one o'clock he met me at my father's office and took me to the Corner Confectionery for lunch. Sometimes I thought I saw Molly swiveling on her stool at the counter, slurping her chocolate malted milkshake. Then I had to ask Bobby to repeat what he'd said.

Friday nights, we went to the movies, and when he drove me home, we stopped in the lane outside town. When he kissed me, he ran a hand beneath my blouse. It was pleasant. My breasts felt full and ripe beneath his hands, and once my fingers strayed to his jeans.

Yet something always held me back.

At night alone in bed, I listened to my heart beat out its dull, distorted rhythm—lub/shhh, lub/shhh—and I thought of Molly dying.

Dr. Wilson said one day my heart would be too weak to pump the blood around my body. "But that will be a long, long time from now," he said. "You should live a long and happy life, but you really shouldn't have children. Labor and delivery would put too much strain on your heart."

Bobby came from a big family—he was the youngest of nine—and he wanted a large brood himself. "We'll have a whole team," he said to me one night.

That night before he left for West Point, I refused his jacket. "We're too young to go steady," I said. "Who knows who we'll meet at school."

After he'd gone, I wished I'd kept the jacket. I had dried the corsage from the prom and taped it to my mirror beneath the photo of the two of us that night. But they were all I had of him. They were all I'd ever have.

Friday, May 6, 1949

Diary dear!

I am helplessly, hopelessly in love! Will—he has asked me to call him Will—is such a dream.

He kissed my hand and said my acting is divine. Then he begged—BEGGED—me to go to Hollywood with him this summer for a screen test. They are making a movie of <u>A Midsummer Dream's Knight</u>, and he wants me to play Gwen! Me. Molly Liddell.

He plans to coach me privately next week.

"Coach you in what?" said cynical Viv. But she has promised to swear I'm at her house rehearsing if Dick tries to track me down. "Don't forget your diaphragm, doll face," she said.

Friday, May 13, 1949

I am <u>si méchante</u>. And it is such fun deceiving Dick. Will invited me to his room at the Gray Star Inn just outside of town. _Il est si charmant. Et moi, je l'aime avec tout mon coeur!_

I was sitting on his bed filing my nails when he took the file away. "Come here, you little minx," he said. He patted his lap, and I straddled his legs and put my arms around his neck.

"Do you really think I could get the part? In the movie, I mean?" I asked. I batted my eyes at him. Naughty Molly.

"Well, that depends." He put his hands on either side of my waist and pinched my skin. "It depends on you, on whether you're willing to do what it takes."

"I'll do whatever you say," I said. "Anything." Diary, I am completely under his spell.

He raised his eyebrows. "Anything?" he said. "Well, we'll see about that. For now" — he tapped the script on the bed beside us —"let's attend to the play. Dearest Gwen, Sir Lance is ready to ride again. What do you say?"

Diary, we read then, together, and the lines never sung to me before like that. We are to practice again tomorrow. Every day for the next week.

I barely noticed Dick this evening. Even when he came to my room, it was as if he was nothing more than the shadow of a bad dream.

Friday, May 20, 1949

Diary,

<u>Enfin!</u> I am escaping from Dick! We had the most dreadful fight tonight. If only he knew where I'd been. He'd strangle me.

Will and I have read the script together every day after school. He is such a genius. I never saw so much in the play—it's so DEEP, unlike the novels of a certain professor I could name. It is about so much more than the end of love between Lance and Gwen. It's about the end of romance, of chivalry, the end of the Old World. Therefore, the end of Dick.

Viv says Will's no better than Dick, that he's just another dirty old man and I'd better watch out, but she's completely wrong. Dick is so *JEALOUS!* If I twirl my spaghetti too enthusiastically, he complains that I care more about pasta than Papa. And he can't stand the way I fall for hot fudge sundaes.

Will, on the other hand, says I'm incredibly seductive. Today he ordered room service—a bottle of Grand Marnier, strawberries and cream. He sat on a chair at the edge of the bed, while I, propped up like a princess on pillows, dipped the berries in the cream and ate them one by one, licking my fingers.

"I could watch you all day," he said. He sat very still, drinking his glass of liqueur—it smells tantalizingly like oranges. "Molly, Ava Gardner has nothing on you. You must keep practicing the exercises I've given you. When you take the next strawberry to your mouth, tip your head back as if you are expecting your lover to kiss you. Yes, like that. Wonderful. Hollywood will throw itself at your feet!"

I don't think my bicycle touched the ground the whole way home!

But, of course, wouldn't you know, that busybody voice teacher Miss Wright had called Dick to ask why I missed my lesson. What an idiot I was not to call her and say I was ill.

After I got back from Will's, I was simply ravenous. (AGAIN! The strawberries must have been enchanted. The kind that make you simply want to beg for more and more and more.) I was devouring the most scrumptious slice of apple pie and thinking Will must taste like that—rather sweet and salty all at once—when Don't-Have-Any-Fun-Without-Me Dick stalked into the kitchen. Where had I been?

"I've been to the moon," I said, closing

my eyes and smiling in the most infuri-
ating Mona Lisa fashion, "and it really is
made of green cheese. Sinfully good, too.
Too bad you missed the trip, _Dad_."

"Molly," said Dick, stalking over and
shaking me by the shoulders, "put down
that fork and wipe that silly grin off
your face. I demand to know where you've
been."

"Silly grin," I said, putting down my
fork and breaking off a bit of pie with
my fingers. "Yes, well, I suppose it is a
silly grin. Probably has something to do
with the lack of gravity in space."

Poor Dick. Dour Dick. Dick detects
deceit on the part of darling Molly.
"Mary Alice, stop playing the fool this
instant. You are not amusing in the
least."

Down, Dick, down. "Why don't you call
Viv and ask her where I've been," I said.

Naturally, he did, the bastard. Of
course Viv knew where I was. I could
hear her on the other end of the line,

laughing as if it was the most moronic question in the world.

"Oh, Dr. Richard," she said. (He simply despises her. She pronounces his name in the French fashion, Dr. Ri-CHARD, but with a deliberately American accent.) "Gwen has spent the entire afternoon with her Lance. You know she is devoted to the play."

I nearly choked! Dick is such a dope. I swallowed the last of my pie, smacked my lips as loudly as I could, and flounced out of the room and into my favorite armchair. I pretended I was sitting in Will's lap. Still deceiving Dick. It is such a glorious game.

He should have been a detective. Not that Viv gave him any satisfaction. "He's so pathetic," she says. "I'm surprised he doesn't check your underwear when you come home."

She doesn't know how pathetic. I've actually caught him sniffing around the laundry hamper.

FINALLY, he hung up and lumbered into the living room.

"Well?" I said, not looking up from my book.

Diary, he flew into the most dreadful rage. He stormed and swore and yanked the stool out from under my feet.

"Cut it out," I said.

He grabbed my book and threw it across the room. "Mary Alice Liddell, sit up straight this instant and tell me exactly where you've been. That story you and your tramp of a friend concocted doesn't fool me in the least."

"Mary Alice Liddell, sit up straight this instant and tell me exactly where you've been," I mimicked.

He was absolutely livid. His face dark red. Veins bulging at his temples. It was quite a show. If I hadn't been so revolted, I would have burst out laughing. Dapper Dick transformed into a grotesque, rotting jack-o'-lantern.

"Take a deep breath and count to

ten," I said and folded my hands on my lap. "You don't want to have a heart attack, _Dad_."

"You're exactly like your mother," he said, frothing at the mouth. "Nothing but a cheap whore. To think of everything I've done for you, lavished on you, and yet you carry on with every drugstore Romeo who wags his finger at you."

Diary, I tried to say something, but he backhanded me across the mouth. "Not another word," he said. "You've seen the last of that play. You're not going to play fast and loose with me."

That was it. I couldn't take it anymore. "Fast and loose!" I screamed. "I was an innocent child when you first molested me beneath my poor mother's very nose. In our very own home. Then, when she sent me away to keep me safe from you, you murdered her. Yes, you did. Don't tell me you didn't. You poisoned her. You kidnapped me. And then you raped me. You raped me and hurt me and made me bleed. I hate you, you bastard, you son of a bitch. You've ruined my life and I hate you for it."

"Molly, don't talk to me like that. I'm warning you." He grabbed my arm and yanked me up out of the chair.

"Go to hell," I said. "Go to hell and rot there. You can't do anything to me."

Then he twisted my arm behind my back—oh, diary, I thought it would BREAK, it hurt so dreadfully—and marched me up to my room and demanded—DEMANDED—that I show him whatever I'd been hiding from him. Letters, money, oh, diary, to think he might have found YOU! He ranted like a madman.

And he might have found you—he held me with one arm and with the other yanked the covers off my bed, shoved the mattress onto the floor, began pulling out all my bureau drawers, ransacking the whole room. He was so close. So close. But then there was a knock at the front door.

Dick hunched downstairs like a guilty gorilla. Mopping his forehead with his starched handkerchief. Panting and wheezing.

It was the paperboy collecting for the month.

Diary, I scarcely knew what I was doing. I simply fled down the stairs and out the door. I hopped on my bike and pedaled as fast as I could, anywhere, away. Away from that hateful, horrible, humping man. I rode all the way to Viv's and I called Will. My White Knight.

Chivalry is not dead. WILL IS HELP-ING ME ESCAPE! We arranged it all over the phone. When I got back home, Dick was beside himself—weeping and pacing.

"Cheer up, Dick," I said. "I am through with that silly play. I am through with school. Take me away from here. I can't stand it anymore." It was one of my best performances. "Everything has gone so terribly wrong. Please, Dad, please take me away."

He agreed. Anything, anything, for his adored, adorable Molly. When he finished swearing his undying love and begging me to forgive him, I even allowed him to carry me upstairs and ravish me. A bittersweet, father-daughter evening. I felt almost sentimental.

Saturday, May 21, 1949

I made Dick promise to let me plan the route for our trip this time. I want to chase butterflies, I told him. I want to Go West. He bobbed and nodded like a marionette. (Dick and his Bobbing Twin. Ever at my beck and call.)

I have barely slept I am so excited. In a mere two days, we will wend our way West, in pursuit of melissa annetta. First we travel to the Grand Canyon. Then on to Utah, where, after Dr.

Richard and his charming stepdaughter check into the Alta Lodge, maria mirabella will spread her wings and fly away.

On Independence Day. A nice touch of symbolism, I think, and heavy-handed like Dick's novels, too.

The plan is this: I will spend one final night with Dick at the Alta Lodge. Eyes, look your last! Arms, take your last embrace! Then, as jocund day stands tiptoe on the misty mountaintops, I shall away, as Will awaits outside my door!

Oh, Will, I will to do thy will. Me thinks we should elope.

Dr. Nabokov, how can I ever thank you?

Dick, after much moping and sighing, agreed to let me spend tonight at Viv's.

"Look, Dick," I said. "You'll have me all to yourself soon enough. You can at least let me say good-bye to my best friend." (Why am I always saying good-bye: Betsy, Chrissy, now Viv.)

"Such a terrific shame," Viv said to Dick when she came to pick me up, "that your work takes you away just before Molly's big debut." Dick said we must tell everyone we are leaving because he is doing research on his next book. "We are all heartbroken. The author most of all. He simply drooled over her. Well, good luck, Dr. Richard." Shaking his hand, "Molly's a great gal. We'll never be able to replace her."

It was such a sad and giddy night. We stole a bottle of champagne from Viv's parents' stash and toasted the future.

"To fame," Viv said, raising her glass. She is going to run away to London and study Shakespeare.

"And fortune," I said. I plan to be frightfully rich as well as famous. Perhaps I'll even convince Warner Brothers to make a movie out of <u>Hunting in the Enchanted Forest</u>. I'll invite Dick to the premiere. What sweet revenge.

To think I'm finally, finally to be free of him.

part three

I, too, was leaving home, but with less sense of freedom and release. Bobby had left for West Point, Nelly for Iowa State University.

The night before I left, Mother came to my room, where I was packing my clothes and books. She took a sweater from my open bureau drawer and began folding it, as she always did, lining up sleeve to sleeve, sleeves flat against the body, then collar to hem.

"Mother," I said. "I can do it myself. I don't want a crease down the middle."

"I know you're feeling anxious," she said, patting my shoulder. "I remember when I first went to college. I was sure the world would never be the same again. And, of course, I was right, but not in the way I imagined. You'll be fine, Betsy."

I refolded the sweater Mother had laid on the bed, in thirds, as the saleswomen did at the dress shops. "Don't try to make me feel better," I said. "You don't understand."

"It's all right," Mother said. She went to the door, then turned back, her hand on the door frame. "Let me know if you want my help."

"I don't want anybody's help," I said. My voice was high and tight, too loud. "And I wish you'd quit saying everything will be all right. You don't know that—no one does."

Mother closed the door quietly. I heard her walk to the living room, say something in a low voice to my father.

I unpacked my trunk and started over again, this time using a cardboard from a gift box in my closet as a guide in folding my blouses and sweaters.

On my shelf was Molly's violet-covered box of journals and treasures. I took it down, clutched it to my chest. I felt her fierceness inside me, felt her defiance in my blood. I packed the box among my books.

In her scrapbook from that spring in Wellesley are a script for *A Midsummer Dream's Knight*, instructions for a series of breathing techniques, and a mimeographed list of mime exercises for beginning actors: "Pretend you open the door and see— your long-lost brother whom you believed died in the War, the boy who stepped on your toes at the homecoming dance, your best friend and her new puppy." "Imagine you are eating—a banana, spare ribs, chicken noodle soup."

Several snapshots of Molly and Viv show them clad in tight-fitting sweaters, knee-skimming skirts, and saddle shoes. Molly with a scarf tied in a jaunty knot around her neck. The girls arm in arm, red-lipped, glossy-haired. Molly inclining her head toward Viv, one arm on her hip, standing before the doors to the school auditorium. The two of them in rolled-up jeans, over-sized white shirts, and penny loafers onstage practicing their lines. Molly hamming it up, raising her skirt and kicking her legs cancan style, blowing kisses at the camera, sticking out her tongue.

There is also a photo of Molly alone, in a wide-shouldered, velvet-collared coat. She is standing on the lawn, one hand in her pocket, the other arm extended and raised. Her fingers are open, reaching, and she gazes upward beyond them. It is almost as if she is oblivious of the photographer, caught in a moment of private wonder.

Perhaps she has sighted a butterfly, one no one else can see.

Wednesday, June 1, 1949

Diary dearest,

The days just seem to drag! Dick is so tiresome. He complained all day about nosy waiters and gas station attendants who ask too many questions and are too solicitous of his Molly.

"No sense of privacy and discretion," sniffed Dick. This from the man who dumps out the contents of my pocketbook every night to make sure I don't have enough change to buy so much as a nail file. (Of course, I've given most of my dough to Will to keep it safe from Dick's dirty digits. YOU I keep hidden in the lining of my valise.)

We're already in Illinois—oh, diary, I so want to see Betsy again, but Dick wouldn't hear of it, and besides, she'd probably despise me now, I am such a juvenile delinquent—so we are passing by some thirty miles south. When Dick stopped for gas this afternoon, a mechanic with Coke-bottle glasses and bad skin gawked at me through the window while he was pumping gas. I stuck my feet up on the dash and started painting my toenails.

"Quite a daughter you've got there," he said to Dick. "I'll bet she drives the boys wild. You must have quite a time keeping her under your thumb."

I pretended I couldn't hear him.

Dick didn't respond. He glared at me and told crater-face to clean the windshield.

After he got back in the car, he said, "I suppose you think it's amusing, tempting every leering Lothario to taste your charms."

"Why don't you go milk a duck, _Dad_," I said, stretching my feet out the window. I reached up beneath my hair and retied my halter top. "You're starting to sound like a broken record."

But Dick ignored his Molly. He cranked up the engine and roared back onto the highway. Poor Dick. His nerves are so jangled. When we finally checked into our motel—same old saggy mattresses, cold showers, and paper-thin walls—he collapsed on the bed and promptly got sloshed.

Sunday, June 12, 1949

Diary,

Dick has been his usual tyrannical self all week. I managed to call Will last Thursday while Dick was out buying me magazines and peppermints. (Plus more gin—he goes through appalling amounts. Dear, departed Mum was a teetotaler by comparison.) Then, just for fun, I necked with the motel owner's son. Very blond and freckled and muscled. Can you imagine, a young hunk in our very own room, fondling Dick's very own Molly on our very own bed!

Dick was quite surly from the time he barged back in—a hangover, no doubt. I had barely begun rummaging through the sacks he plunked down on the table before he began accusing me of various crimes against the state. I am convinced he was a member of the Spanish Inquisition in a past life. To say nothing of what he might have taught the Gestapo.

Why was I smirking like that? Why was my lipstick smeared? What was that stain on the bedspread? Would I please account for every minute of the past hour and a half!

"Well, let's see, _Dad_," I said, putting my chin on my hand. "Gee, first I flushed some love notes down the toilet. Then a vampire bit me on the leg. Here, do you want to see?" I offered him my leg, where I'd scratched open a mosquito bite, but he smacked it away.

"Molly, I won't have you play the fool. I want a straight account immediately," said Dick.

"Gee, sorry," I said. I folded my hands on my lap. "Don't get so hot under the collar. Okay, let me see. Oh, yeah, then a mysterious man slipped into our room and ravished me right here on the bed. That must be where the stain came from." I smiled like an angel.

Well, diary, you know the rest. Dick has already destroyed two of my favorite blouses in a frenzy. Of course, he is always SO sorrowful afterward that he buys me three more for every one he ruins. I can barely close my suitcase, and we have only been on the road for three weeks.

Monday, June 13, 1949

The first of my butterflies! A perfect specimen of <u>Oarisma powesheik</u>. A rather plain yellow-brown skipper, but a true WESTERN species. I am sure it is an omen. Will's convertible is yellow. He let me drive it back in Wellesley, sitting on his lap. Twenty-one days till we drive off into the Salt Lake City sunrise!

I can't wait to be rid of Dick. He is such a leech, and on the road, there is nowhere to avoid him. The only time he leaves me alone is when I'm lepping. Naturally, he's jealous of my butterflies, because they deprive him of heavy breathing poolside while I splash around and show off my legs and tummy. But he much prefers I tramp around in baggy jeans and T-shirt in a meadow far away from strangers, so I am on my own while he sits in the car, hunched over his writing tablet. (He has not had much success lately—many crumpled pages— which does not improve his temperament.)

I miss Viv. I had forgotten how dreary it is with only Dick for company.

But in a week we shall be at the Grand Canyon.

$\mathcal{A}$ at last I was to satisfy my own wanderlust. In summer of 1957, as a college graduation present, Grandma Keckler took me to Paris. Bobby Baker had become engaged, and I was grateful for the diversion.

In preparation for our trip, Grandma and I pored over maps of the city, plotted excursions to Versailles, Les Tuilleries, Le Louvre, Le Musée d'Orsay, L'Arc de Triomphe, Notre Dame, Le Sacré Coeur. Here Hemingway and Fitzgerald had dined. There Grandma had lived. Here was where Marie Antoinette had kept her perfumed sheep and pretended to be a shepherdess.

Grandma and I stayed in modest lodgings on the Rive Gauche and sauntered along the banks of the Seine, scouting for bargains at the old booksellers' booths. It was there, on a pale blue morning when the far bank of the river was shrouded in fog, that I found a tattered copy of the fables of La Fontaine, which Grandma had taught Molly and me when we were young. I could still recite *"La cigale et la formi,"* and had I been the ant, I surely would have fed the grasshopper, for she sang so beautifully.

In the afternoon, we climbed the tiers of stairs to Sacré Coeur, at the summit of Mont Martre, resting now and then when I grew short of breath. The exertion was worth it. From the top, a sea of beige buildings and slate-blue rooftops spread out below me. A fine mist was falling, and the prism of rain refracted the sun and cast a rainbow over the city.

In bed that night, I dreamed I stood again on Mont Martre, high above Paris, the arc of yellow, green, and lilac stretching from one end of the city to the other. From below, sightseers climbed in knots of three and four, sometimes a child alone sprinting ahead of her parents. One girl in particular vaulted forward, three steps at a time, as if she were Mercury himself reinvented as a goddess. It was Molly. She waved to me, her cheeks flushed from the climb, shouting something I could not hear. She still wore braids, the tangled braids I had adored, now glinting almost red in the misty Paris sun. My Molly. The Molly who had never met Dick Richard, had never lost her heart to William Tennessee.

I strained to catch her words, but as I leaned into the wind, she began to fade. The sky darkened and a gray drizzle descended on the city. Molly called to me again, grinning, still running up the stairs, but as she drew closer, she became diaphanous and blurred. Was it the rain, the setting sun, that obscured her from my vision? In the Paris gloam, I saw her one last instant, arms and legs suspended in midair, and in that moment I thought I heard her call my name. "Betsy!"

But she had disappeared.

she had disappeared, escaped from Dick. It was July Fourth, just as she had planned. On the lupine-scented slopes near the Alta Lodge, she ran away with Will. She would see Dick just once more, three years hence.

From the beginning, there was friction between Molly and

Will. He pointed the yellow convertible East, both Las Vegas and Hollywood receding into the distance with each passing mile. Molly and he had not yet made love. She had tired of his voyeuristic foreplay. "I am beginning to think," she wrote one night when he deserted her at dinner and failed to return till the next morning, "that he doesn't love me after all. What a goose I have been. He probably made up the bit about the film contract for *A Midsummer Dream's Knight*, too. I am as hopeless as Mummy ever was!"

She confronted Will, dry-eyed and trembling. Yes, he said, of course he loved her. And no, he had not lied about the film contract. In fact, because of the great degree of artistic control the studio had given him over the movie, the initial screen tests were to be conducted, not in Hollywood, but at his own estate back in the Hamptons.

Molly sulked. She longed for palm trees and premieres, for stars that left the heavens to walk upon the earth. But if they were to film the movie itself in Los Angeles, she would endure screen tests in New York—for him, because she loved him. For she did love him, with a desperation that alarmed her. She had considered herself above love—it was nonsense, just as the physical act itself was nothing more than evolution's way of mocking humankind. We were no better than the great apes. She knew that, or thought she did. Now she was not sure.

For the first time in her life, Molly was a captive to the strange chemical reactions that ruled her body and dictated her emotions. Before, it was she who had summoned them forth, who had allowed herself to fall under their spell. But she had always banished them at will. And she had long ago ceased to feel anything but indifference and repulsion, sometimes even pity, toward Dick.

Dick. Dick was another puzzle. From time to time, she almost missed him. He was such a sap. Such a romantic sap. Will scoffed at all that slosh. And now Molly found herself under the sway of those same dreary sentiments that she had despised in Dick.

By the time she and Will reached the Hamptons, she feared the worst, hoped only to salvage a bit part in the movie, something to take her to Los Angeles, where she would make her own way, start again.

Will owned a ten-bedroom mansion that looked out across the bay. A boardwalk led to a small sandy beach, with a dock and a faded blue-and-white rowboat. Molly remembered the estate. She and Chrissy had visited it that first summer after Molly had moved East. The girls had been awestruck by the glorious decadence of it all—the tidal pool complete with sea urchins and starfish in the great room, the whirlpool in the master bath, the private theater with reclining seats big enough to hold two people at once.

There were seven other teens living there, all chaperoned by a woman who served their meals in silence, then retreated to the nether regions of the house. That first night, Will invited Molly to the whirlpool. When she arrived, two boys, naked, their knees breaking through the rippling surface of the water, were already seated in the tub. Will told her to undress and sit between them. He gave directions to the boys, sat across from them, and watched. Molly left the room.

In response, Will took her to the private theater and showed her his films. He told her what she would do the next day when he began filming again. Told her he would throw her out if she refused to participate.

She ran out of the house, down to the beach, and rowed the boat out, out, across the black water, away from the house. The stars shone false and bright. She rowed on till her arms were as numb as her heart. She sat for hours, the wind rocking the boat and pushing it ever farther away from shore. The bay was ringed with shrubs and grasses which whispered to her, "Leave him. Leave him."

Molly listened to the whispering leaves, imagined herself evergreen, everblue. In the morning, she awoke stiff and groggy, her head resting on her arms. She was seated on the floor of the little boat, her tingling legs curled beneath her. Her arms were folded across the rough, wooden seat. She picked at the splinters in her skin, winced at the pinpricks of blood that welled to the surface. She was starved, longed for pancakes smothered in strawberries and chocolate sauce. She decided to leave Will that morning.

She swam back to shore, leaving his boat adrift in the bay, packed up her belongings again, and stole his car. "He has others," she wrote, "and besides, he owes me this one."

Diary,

I don't know what to do. I'm staying with another girl who ran away from Will. I'm not the only one he promised to make into a movie star. I am such a dope.

Sarah says we should hit the road and set out for Hollywood ourselves, but neither one of us has any money.

"We can waitress," she said. "Or if that doesn't work, we can always work the hotels where we stay. It's not like we don't know how to give a blow job. We might as well earn money for it."

Sarah is so hard and cold. I wonder if I'm like that now.

Maybe I should just go back to Wellesley and see if I can stay with Viv. Or try to track down Chrissy, or even long-lost Betsy. What would Betsy think of me, hanging out with a girl who doesn't care if she's a prostitute?

No matter what, I promise I won't do that. That would be giving in to Dick and Will, saying, Yes, that's all I'm good for.

I am so hungry. Sarah and I split a cheeseburger today, and I bought a jar of pickles. Sweet gherkins. I ate them all and drank the pickle juice.

> Monday, August 22, 1949

Diary dear,

My first day of work as a waitress. My feet ache! I am writing lying on the floor with my feet propped up on a chair.

Sarah left for New York City yesterday. She says she's going to be a model. I am rooming with another waitress named Annie. We live in a basement apartment, and there is a little window above my bed that looks out on a window well. If I lie at the foot of the bed and hang my head over the side, I can see the sky.

I have a closet with a light in it and a chest of drawers painted white with yellow and blue pansies. I put my butter-flies on top and smile at them before I go to sleep.

After we're through with our shift—we work from six p.m. to midnight—we can have a meal in the kitchen. Tonight I had a club sandwich and fruit cocktail.

Saturday, September 24, 1949

DEAR MOLLY,

Hi. I'm here in New York City, living with a photographer I met at a shoot. I haven't got a job yet, but he's helping me put together a portfolio to take around to the agencies. I've dyed my hair blond, and I paint a beauty mark on my cheek each morning.

Gary is such fun. We go out every night to little jazz clubs in the Village. Usually we shoot some smack beforehand. Have you tried it? It's such a rush.

I thought you might get a kick out of the enclosed from this morning's New York Times. What goes around comes around, huh?

How do you like the pix of Miss Liberty on the other side? We were going to take the ferry to see her yesterday, but we didn't have the energy. We don't get up till noon, and there's never anything but peanut butter in the cupboard.

Write back, Molly, and do come see us. I'll take you to Tiffany's, and we can pick out the diamonds we'll wear when we receive our Academy Awards.

SWEETS TO THE SWEET,
SARAH

The New York Times, *Saturday, September 24, 1949*

Tornado Spawned by Tropical Storm Mary Damages Playwright's Estate

SOUTHAMPTON, N.Y. —The estate of William Tennessee, noted playwright and winner of a Tony for his latest play, *A Midsummer Dream's Knight*, was destroyed last night in a tornado spawned by Tropical Storm Mary, which hovered off the coast yesterday.

The tornado, which caused no other damage in the Hamptons, touched down shortly before midnight in Shinnecock Bay and created a water spout that destroyed a wooden rowboat and dock before advancing to the house, where it tore off the roof of the main house and demolished a carriage house at the back of the property.

Tennessee was not at home and could not be reached for comment. However, a housekeeper said the twister resulted in the destruction of all the upstairs bedrooms, the kitchen, and a private theater. No estimate of the damages was available by press time.

Police are investigating the presence of a number of juveniles in the house who are not related to Tennessee. The juveniles have been taken to an undisclosed location and are under the care of social workers, who hope to return them to their families.

over the next year, Molly moved around frequently. She no longer had a car. She had sold the convertible she'd taken from Will after she and Sarah parted. She hitchhiked. Sometimes, when she'd saved enough in tips, she bought a bus ticket. At first she took jobs as a waitress, lifeguard, stable hand at resorts and country clubs in Vermont, Cape Cod, and upstate New York, hoping to meet someone who could spark her career.

But as time passed, she no longer dreamed of Hollywood or Broadway. "I am tired of sucking up to lechers and buffoons," she wrote in the summer of 1950. Although the tips were smaller, she gravitated to country inns and roadside diners. "I like the people," she told her diary. "They make me laugh."

Wherever she worked, she lived in cramped apartments and trailers with other waitresses she met on the job. Some had boyfriends who slept over. Some tried to sleep with her. Others tried to fix her up with friends. She refused them all.

On her days off, when the weather was fine, Molly walked. She tramped through fields of Queen Anne's lace and cornflowers, goldenrod and milkweed. She skipped stones at the edge of a lake, took off her shoes and waded into the icy water, balancing on smooth stones slippery with algae. Sometimes she took her diary and wrote by a waterfall. Often she took her butterfly net with her. She caught very few specimens; there were few to be found. She lamented the fact that she had never discovered *melissa annetta* during her short stay at the Alta Lodge.

The mood of the country had changed again. The euphoria

of the Allied victory had subsided, and the specter of nuclear holocaust, the Communist threat, hovered in the air, like smog. The United States had begun to dispatch troops to South Korea, and Molly remembered Lieutenant Johnson. Remembered him crying on her mother's knees. She waited on boys who were being shipped out, let them take her to the movies, undress her in the backseats of their Oldsmobiles and Chevys. They wept like babies, their tears soaking her blouse. She kissed their salt-caked eyelashes. She held them to her breast and rocked them.

There was one boy in particular. His hair was pale as winter wheat, his blue eyes paler still. His fingers were cold and soft as baby's skin. When he touched Molly's breasts, she felt as if she were being fondled by a ghost. The boy's father had fought in the war. He had served in Okinawa, been captured and forced to march at gunpoint by the Japanese. The Japanese shot anyone who fell out of line. His father's best friend had stumbled. They left him dead in the road and marched on. The pale boy, whose name Molly never asked—she refused to let any of them tell her their names, called them all "dear" and "honey"—had taken a bottle of pills so he wouldn't have to go to war. His uncle had found him and rushed him to the hospital, where they pumped out his stomach and sent him home.

Unlike the others, he didn't cry. He held her hand in an icy grip and stared straight ahead, out the windshield, into the blackness. She lay back on the seat, lifted her skirt, slipped off her panties, and pulled him on top of her. Afterward, he fell asleep, his withered penis still inside her. She lay awake all night beneath him, kept her arms and legs curled around his slack body. "Asleep," she wrote, "he seemed more substantial. I could feel the weight of him, pressing me to earth. As if I were all that was between him and the grave." In the morning, she took him to the diner where she worked and brought him pancakes, bacon, eggs, and coffee. He reported for duty the next day. She never saw or heard from him again.

It was Christmas Eve 1950. Four days later, *Time* magazine named the "U.S. Fighting Man" as its "Man of the Year."

When Molly saw the cover, she thought of the boy and wept.

Once the tears began to fall, she could not stop them. She wept for her father, her brother, her long-lost friends, forgotten dreams.

She wept even for her mother. "Poor Mum," she wrote in a faint and shaky hand. "How sad her life was."

i was angry that Molly, who had brought me back to life, was so accepting of her fate. Molly, who had kicked a skater for me, refused Tommy DiFelice, run away from Dick, then Will. Now it seemed that each boy who entered her and emptied himself took away, in place of his own desperation, one more molecule of her vitality.

She wrote little of these boys. She recorded their favorite

foods—French fries and vinegar, banana splits with pineapple topping, even liver and onions. She jotted down whether they were in the Army, Navy, or Marines, the date they shipped out, their destination. She noted whether their big toes were larger than their second toes.

Each time I read these lines, I saw Molly falling, falling— falling again and again beneath the succession of bodies that pressed her down and smothered her. Each time, she resurfaced a little paler, a little more translucent, till it was as if she were an X ray, phosphorescent bones inside rice-paper skin, silent as atomic ash.

molly grew pale, translucent, but she had a radioactive half-life that continued to burn inside me. In 1978, on the eve of my twenty-fifth high-school class reunion, I dragged out my old yearbook and scanned the faces of my friends. Leonelle Trilling. Esther Rachel Freeman. Hazel Marie Kowalsky. But Mary Alice Liddell was missing.

My own face smiled back at me, tentative but hopeful. The photo was taken the summer before my senior year, before Molly died, before I became ill.

The caption beneath read:

"Hoops heroine . . . '52 league championship MVP . . . brawny, brainy . . . future lawyer . . . First Woman Supreme Court Justice?"

I imagined what the caption beneath Molly's picture would have said:

"Thespian par excellence . . . jitterbugger . . . mad scientist . . . mad about malteds . . . Broadway bound."

I kept my promise to Molly, and to myself. I did graduate from Harvard Law School. But from there I went not to Washington, D.C., but to Chicago, where I clerked for a juvenile court judge. When Mother died, I returned home to care for Father and joined his firm. With me I brought the memory of a twelve-year-old girl who'd been convicted of shoplifting lipstick and perfume. Her name was Susan, and she had reddish brown hair like Molly's. She was a hooker, and after her detention, she was strangled by her pimp.

By now I understood what Dick had done to Molly, what had happened to so many girls I'd met and counseled. With my father's blessing, I founded the Charleston Women's Legal Aid Services. Seven of us, men and women, worked nights pro bono preparing cases for women whose husbands had beaten or abandoned them, for mothers who sought to save their children from abuse. I was shocked we had so many clients in our quiet little town.

Like my mother, grandmother, and great-grandmother before me, I earned a reputation as a firebrand for women's rights. I liked my label as "libber," and as I dressed for the class reunion, I selected a pair of wide-legged navy satin pants with matching satin top and chunky, high-heeled pant boots. When I met Bobby Baker that night, I shook his hand beneath the mirror ball and nodded to his petite and miniskirted wife.

"Here's a photo of our kids," he shouted over the music, leaning toward my ear. He held out a picture of three children, a boy about sixteen, who looked just like his father but with long hair, and two girls, somewhere between eight and eleven, one with braces. Their hair, too, was long and parted in the middle.

"They're charming," I said, smiling first at Mrs. Baker, then at Bobby.

"Excuse me," he shouted. "I can't hear you over all this racket. It sounds just like the stereo in Bobby Junior's bedroom. Kids today. Were we ever that bad?"

He wore his officer's dress whites—he was still in the military—uniform and contact lenses that tinted his eyes an artificial blue, and as I drove home that night, I wondered what would have happened had I married him. I found I was not sorry I had not, though I found, as well, that I still had tender feelings for him.

 in the fall of 1951, Molly met her husband, Robert Porter. At nineteen, he had left his family in Colorado to try to make his way in upstate New York. He had dreamed of starting his own construction business—suburban homes were sprouting everywhere like dandelions. He had become the foreman for an outfit based in Rochester and had bought used business management and accounting texts from the university bookstore and studied nights at home, over burgers and beer.

At twenty-one, he was sent to Korea. He shipped out with Maj. Gen. William Dean's advance battalion, the 24th Infantry Division, and landed in Pusan on July 1, 1950. He never saw any action, but his hearing was damaged when he contracted a severe secondary ear infection in connection with a bout of malaria.

Something snapped inside. He began having nightmares, waking up feverish and shouting. One night he ran off into the jungle in his skivvies, waving his rifle over his head. They sent him back to the States, to the V.A. Hospital in Washington, D.C. When he was released, only ten months after he had shipped overseas, he made his way back to Rochester. But the foreman's job was long gone. Besides, he could no longer hear. You had to shout at him. And his nerves were bad.

He took a job in Syracuse washing dishes at a diner where Molly waitressed. They went out for burgers after work. She asked his name. They shared a beer; he shared his past. "I told him not to ask about my own," she wrote. "I told him my dad and brother died when I was a kid, my mother the summer I was twelve. I told him I had a stepfather, but I hadn't seen or heard from him in ages. I said I didn't want to talk about it."

He said that was just fine. He took her hand.

Tuesday, September 11, 1951

Dear diary,

Bob has asked me to marry him. Me, who swore I'd never marry.

I said yes. It will be a civil ceremony, just us and Sally, the hostess at Sam's Shakes and Fries, as our witness. The manager, Joe Finelli, is giving us a week off. We don't have any money, but Bob is good at making and fixing things. We're going to save up and buy a house.

I guess you wonder why I am marrying him. Well, he's kind, for one thing. And he's damaged, just like me.

We're made for each other. Besides, he loves me, and he needs me. I told him I'm not a virgin. He said it doesn't matter. He wants to wait till we are married.

this new Molly was a puzzle. Her diary entries were shorter, more subdued. The exclamation points and capital letters had disappeared. She no longer lapsed into French. A typical entry was "The daisies along the road are blooming. I picked a bouquet for the table." Or "We had a terrible thunderstorm last night. Isn't it funny, thunder doesn't frighten me anymore?"

Once, sitting beside a stream, she wrote of her disappointment that she and Bob had no money for a plane trip to see his folks in Colorado. Then: "I have come to believe that second best, next to flying, is wanting to fly."

When I read these entries as a girl, I saw only resignation and defeat in her words, the choices she had made. Jane Eyre with her blind Mr. Rochester, Aurora Leigh with her blind Romney. I was sure I could not be content with such a man, with such a life. I was sure that Molly had, at last, betrayed herself.

bob and molly left New York for Pennsylvania, then West Virginia. She waitressed. He attempted and abandoned a succession of odd jobs. Carpentry. Welding. Garbage collection. Construction again. Nothing lasted, and the little money they had ran out.

They moved to a two-room house at the end of a dusty lane on the outskirts of town and adopted an old gray tomcat who showed up on their doorstep one morning, thin and cringing. Molly named him Galahad.

Bob found a job in the coal mines. He lost it.

Molly got pregnant. When she could no longer stomach the smell of food, she had to quit her job at the diner.

Bob scared up a job delivering newspapers, but it paid very little. Most carriers then were boys of ten or twelve, their wages sufficient for a soda or a movie.

Still, Molly stood by him with a constancy that reminded me of our childhood friendship. Molly was loyal. She had always been so.

Now and then, she read news of Dick, who had published a new novel called *The Truth About Wonderland*. She did not read it.

Friday, August 1, 1952

Dear diary,

Bob and I are leaving tomorrow for Denver. His parents have sent us money for train fare, and his brother got him a job in the mines.

I am so happy. At first we'll live with Bob's mom and dad, but, diary, I hope one day we'll have a house of our own, with a room for the baby. I'm sure she's going to be a girl, and she's going to have the best of everything. Dance and drama lessons. Girl Scouts. Maybe I'll become a scout leader. I know something of butterflies, and I'm not afraid of spiders. Besides, I can canoe and swim. And I've got heaps of songs to sing around the campfire.

Tuesday, September 23, 1952

Dearest diary,

You won't believe it. I saw Dick today. And he has given us ever so much dough. Enough to buy a house.

He was giving a reading at the
library, and I went to hear him.

Diary, it was so strange seeing him
again. He looked so old. He had great,
dark circles under his eyes, and his
clothes hung on him. He was still
handsome, of course, and well dressed.
Dick was always well dressed, even for an
afternoon of debauching his Molly. But he
had shrunk somehow.

"Molly," he said and shook my hand.

"I don't have any money to buy a book,
Dad," I said. "I just wanted to say hi."

He was staring at my belly, as if he
was revolted. Disgusted at how far his
Molly had fallen.

"It's okay, Dad," I said. "I'm going to
have a baby."

He waved me to a seat. "Wait," he said,
"until I'm through, and we can go to
lunch."

He took me to a restaurant—the best as
always.

Can you believe it? He was mooning

over me, after all this time. He grilled
me about how I had escaped, as if he still
had control over me. He never guessed.
He thought <u>Bob</u> kidnapped me. Dear,
innocent Bob, who knows nothing about any
of it.

Then he tried to get the whole story
out of me. Still the snoop. Where was
Will? What had I done with him? What
had he done with me?

"I'm not going to tell you anything at
all," I said. I couldn't believe he could
still make me so angry. "I loved Will," I
said. "It doesn't matter what he did to
me. It's nothing compared to what you
did. If that's the only reason you invited
me to lunch, I'm leaving. I don't have to
take this anymore."

"What about Bob?" he asked, signaling
the waiter for another glass of wine. "What
about your husband?"

"I'm happy with Bob," I said. "He loves
me, which is more than I can say for you
or Will."

He started to cry. He put his head down on his hands and cried like a baby. Bob's love was nothing to his, Dick's, love. He had always loved me, he would love me forever. He would never love anyone else. Please, please, please, would I leave Bob and run away with him?

As if we'd been lovers, as if we'd quarreled, and now he wanted to make it up.

I put down my fork. "I'll never go anywhere with you," I said. "I'd go back to Will before I'd go back to you. If you don't stop this, I'm walking right out that door."

"No, don't, Molly." He reached over and put his hand over mine. When I cringed, he pulled it back.

"Look," he said. "I've tried and tried to find you. If you won't come back to me, at least let me give you this." He took out his checkbook and wrote out a check for FOUR THOUSAND BUCKS!

"I don't want a thing from you," I said. "Bob and I will be just fine."

I wiped my mouth with my napkin, very ladylike.

"It's not my money," he said, waving at the check. "It's yours by right. It's rent money from the house in Ithaca. If you give me your address, I'll have my lawyer write to you and arrange for you to receive the money every month."

"No strings attached?" I didn't trust him. "I don't want you to try to stay in touch with me. I don't want you begging Bob or me to see my daughter."

"No strings," he said. He lowered his eyes and dabbed at them with a handkerchief.

Diary, I was so overwhelmed. I went straight to the bank. Money from our old house on Seneca Street. It must have included the rent from Dr. Nabokov and his wife. I never wrote to him, to thank him for the advice on the butterflies.

Bob was so thrilled. "I thought you said you didn't get along with your stepdad," he said. "He seems like a swell guy to me."

"Yes," I said. "He's a swell guy. Too bad he didn't know how to raise a daughter."

Bob sat down on the couch beside me. "Do you want to talk about it?" he asked.

I took his hand and placed it on my stomach. "Feel," I said. "She's kicking. I think she's going to be a dancer."

Bob understood. He didn't ask again.

I need to put it all behind me now. What's past is not prologue.

A what's past may not be prologue, but it is present always.

I have a secret, one that I have never shared.

I, too, saw Dick, once while I was at law school. In Boston, I felt so near to Molly. Weekends, I sometimes went to Wellesley and walked the streets. I saw her strolling down Central Street, arm in arm with Viv, chewing her gum with furious intensity and shrieking with laughter at some private joke. I stopped at the drugstore and saw her seated at the counter, slurping down a malted milkshake, or jitterbugging across the floor with Craig, her saddle shoes a blur of black and white.

One day, it was just before Thanksgiving, I went to Dr. Richard's office. I had bought his book and taken it with me as a pretext.

He looked up from his reading when I knocked. "May I help you?" he asked, removing his reading glasses. I was startled by his British accent, even though I knew he had gone to school abroad. He did look like Alan Ladd, aging now, but he was still a hunk, as Molly would have said.

I had never wanted to kill anyone before. But as I watched his hands straightening the papers on his desk, I wanted to strangle him, though not before I had cut off his genitals. Those hands had mauled my childhood friend.

He pointed to a chair. "Now, what can I do for you?" he asked. "I don't remember seeing you in class."

"I'm not in class," I said. My voice was flat and calm. I did not recognize it.

"You've read my book, I see. Tell me, what do you think of it? Be truthful now." He crossed his legs and folded his hands over his knees in a gesture of good humor veiling mild annoyance.

"I have," I said. "And I think I do know the truth about Wonderland. In fact, I'm sure I do."

He straightened then and leaned a little closer. "What do you mean?"

I took a deep breath and plunged on, quickly now before I lost my nerve. "I know the truth about you and your step-daughter, Molly Liddell. I know you raped her, I know she ran away from you."

His face darkened. "What do you know?" he asked in a low voice.

"She told me everything. About you, about William Tennessee. I'm prepared to go to the board of trustees here at the college unless you quit. I don't think they want a child molester teaching their coeds."

"How do I know you're telling the truth?" he asked. He had turned very pale and was clutching at his chest.

"Because I told you. I know the truth about Wonderland. Don't test me on this, Dick."

Two weeks later, there was a story in the *Boston Globe* about Dr. Richard Richard resigning his teaching post at Wellesley to pursue his career as a novelist. A second story followed on New Year's Day. The year was 1960. I was home on break and read it in the *Charleston Gazette*.

The Charleston Gazette, *Friday, January 1, 1960*

Author Shoots Prize-Winning Playwright in New Year's Eve Brawl

Southampton, N.Y.—Dr. Richard Richard, best-selling author of *Hunting in the Enchanted Forest* and *The Truth About Wonderland,* pleaded guilty to attempted murder last night after a New Year's Eve brawl with Tony-winning playwright William Tennessee at the latter's estate.

Guests scattered when Richard crashed the party shortly after 11 P.M. and brandished a gun, shouting, "You traitor, you'll pay for this." When Tennessee tried to calm him down and offered him a drink, sources at the scene revealed, Richard shot him once in the chest at close range. Richard then asked for the telephone and called the police himself.

Ambulance personnel rushed Tennessee to Charles and Dorothy Hays Memorial Hospital, where he is listed in guarded condition. Hospital spokesman Morgan L. Fay said the bullet grazed one lung and lodged in the spinal cord. Although a team of surgeons successfully removed the bullet, Tennessee is paralyzed from the waist down. Fay said doctors will not speculate on his chances for recovery. "It's simply too soon to tell," she said. "Mr. Tennessee is receiving the best medical care possible, and that is all I can and will say."

Richard was arraigned at 1 A.M. this morning before District Justice Sherwood Lott and entered a guilty plea to attempted murder. He refused to give a motive for his actions.

Speculation today centers on professional jealousy. Tennessee, whose play *A Midsummer Dream's Knight* was made into a movie by Warner Brothers last year, reportedly encouraged the studio to turn down an offer from Richard's agent for the screen rights to *Hunting in the Enchanted Forest.*

Richard quit his job as professor of literature at Wellesley College, Mass., at the close of the fall semester to devote himself full-time to his writing.

Following his arraignment, Richard was transferred to the New York State Penitentiary, where he has been placed under a suicide watch. Sentencing is scheduled for next month after a psychiatric evaluation.

The Boston Globe, *Tuesday, February 2, 1960*

AUTHOR SENTENCED TO LIFE IN PRISON
FOR ATTEMPTED MURDER

ALBANY, N.Y.—Best-selling author Richard
Richard was sentenced yesterday to life in prison for
the attempted murder of playwright William Tennessee
in East Hampton, New York, on New Year's Eve.

Richard, 48, was returned to the New York State
Penitentiary immediately after sentencing by Judge
Morton Arthur. As he has since his arrest, Richard,
who was deemed sane following a psychiatric
evaluation, refused to give a motive for the shooting.
"I'm clearly guilty," he told Judge Arthur before a
packed courtroom. "If I had the chance, I'd shoot him
again. Only this time I'd be sure I killed him."
Richard smiled serenely as guards led him away in
handcuffs after sentencing. He has refused all requests
for interviews by the media.

Tennessee remains paralyzed from the waist down
following the New Year's attack at his Hamptons
estate. Once his condition stabilized, he was moved
last month from the Charles and Dorothy Hays
Memorial Hospital to an undisclosed private facility,
where he is undergoing intensive and painful physical
therapy, according to his agent, Kevin Harper.

Richard, the author of *The Truth About Wonderland,* has not written a new novel in eight years. He had just resigned his teaching post at Wellesley College, Mass., before crashing a party at Tennessee's estate and shooting the Tony-winning playwright at close range.

Fans of both Richard and Tennessee kept vigil outside the courthouse during sentencing, and police stood by to prevent outbreaks of violence in the unruly crowd. No one was arrested.

Sunday, December 21, 1952

Dear diary,

Only four more days till Christmas. Bob and I went to church this morning, and I could barely waddle down the aisle. I am huge. I can't wait for little Betsy to be born.

The house looks gorgeous. Bob cut down a tree, and we decorated it Saturday night. We made a construction paper garland in red and gold and covered milk bottle caps with foil and pasted pictures of each member of the family in one and hung them on the tree. I even found some old photos of Mum and Dad, and Saint Michael. One of Betsy, too, because we're still blood sisters, and besides, diary, can you believe it, she's going to be the baby's godmother!

Thursday, December 25, 1952

Merry Christmas, diary,

I am so exhausted. We got up and

went to Bob's parents' house this morning before church. His mom even knitted a stocking for me and for the baby. They gave us a stroller and a bassinet.

Bob's mom taught me to knit, too, and I made Bob a pair of argyle socks. One is a little longer than the other, but he was so sweet, he put them on right away.

I think I ate too much mincemeat pie. Little Betsy is restless tonight. She keeps kicking like she's jitterbugging back and forth inside my stomach. I suppose she'll torment me the way I tormented poor old Mum.

I haven't slept much the past week. I suppose it's the excitement.

I tried to go to sleep, but I kept hearing the choir singing in church this morning, "For unto us a child is born." Bob, the lamb, sleeps like a baby himself.

It can't be long now. Baby Jesus, please help me to be a good mother to little Betsy.

for years, whenever I thought of Molly, I struggled to make sense of what had happened to her. I know now what I could not have known when I was young—that even had I told my mother about Mrs. Liddell, about Lieutenant Johnson and Tommy DiFelice, Molly's fate most likely would have been the same. Mrs. Liddell would have left Charleston for Ithaca to escape the scandal. Molly would have been kidnapped, raped, and run away. The end would have been the same—death, death, death.

I know now, too, that Will's paralysis and Dick's imprisonment will never bring me peace.

And so I am left, always, with the same question: How do you celebrate a life of diminished possibilities, diminished expectations? For many years, I had no answer. For many years, I only saw what might have been, what should have been.

And yet, in my old age, I've finally learned what Molly herself discovered long ago. I see it in her dreams for her daughter. In the daisies she picked for her table. The quiet love she found in Bob.

Molly herself gave me the answer to my question. Now when I read those last entries, her final letter to me, I am struck by the lack of bitterness. She is elated. She and Bob are rich. They have a home. She has in-laws who dote on her. She is eager to be a mother, eager to teach her daughter canoeing and dance and singing. Eager to tell her stories about the past.

I wonder sometimes which stories she would tell.

I would tell the one about the time we went ice-skating. Or

maybe the times we helped Mrs. Liddell entertain the soldiers. I would certainly tell about the nights we spent searching for enemy planes with Dr. Liddell, about dancing with Dem Bones, and dissecting frogs. In time, maybe I would tell about Tommy DiFelice. I think I would tell about how it felt to dance with Molly, to ride Tommy's motorcycle.

I would tell about what it is to be a girl, to experience the strange and reckless sensations that grip you like the flu—the flushed face, weak knees, the vertigo. I would tell what it is like to be held captive by a glance, a touch—and at the same time to find yourself a queen, able to command the world with the flick of a finger, the bat of an eye.

I would say that a girl should never give up those feelings, nor the glamour of a goddess that descends on her, surrounds her like a mantle—that she should cling to them, for they are hers by birthright. That she should not have to become a tree, a cow, a flute. A girl should become a woman, whose body has blossomed even as her blood has sung to her, sung of its own rhythms and longings, its secret pleasures and delights.

My life, unlike Molly's, has been long and blessed. After my father died, I became the senior partner in his law firm. I have lived well, done good work. Spent summers in France, winters, too, sometimes.

And lately, though I've never married, I've begun to see a poet. I never trusted poets. I never trusted lawyers, either, or businessmen or academics.

The poet is seventy-two and walks with a lion-headed cane.

He wears worn corduroys, shiny at the knees, and tweed jackets with suede patches at the elbows. He smokes a pipe. His hands are coarse—not the hands of a poet, not pale, fine fingers, but short ones, ruddy and cracked, like sausages. He is blind without his glasses and forgets the time, sometimes the day, we've agreed to meet.

I forgive him. I hold his hand in the dark of the theater. Sometimes he parks the car in the drive and unbuttons my coat, slips his hand beneath my blouse. Then I tug at his shirttail, run my fingers along the band of his trousers. His soft, gray fur tickles my hand. I can feel the ripple in his belly, answering the ripple in my own.

I brush off his suggestions that he move in with me, that we economize and merge our households. But I have considered inviting him to stay the night. Perhaps I will. Tomorrow.

When I let myself into the house after he drops me off, I see Molly sitting on the kitchen stool, slurping a cherry Coke and downing an enormous slice of apple pie. She takes in the hem of my blouse escaping from my waistband, the stray hairs at my forehead. I know she knows the rest.

I smile at her, then look away, embarrassed.

She puts down her fork and grins. "It's about time, Betsy," she says. She pushes her curls back over her shoulders and tucks one leg beneath her. "There's nothing wrong with it, you know, when two people love each other."

"What do you mean?" I ask, knowing at last what Molly has

always known, what Molly has never forgotten no matter what her fate.

She grins at me, rolls her eyes. "Betsy," she says, "you look drunk."

"I only had one glass of wine," I say. "Just one at dinner." I hold my coat around me like a shield.

"Ce n'est pas le vin," she says. "You're crazy about him, aren't you? He makes your heart beat fast."

"He's a nice man," I say. I want to confide in her, but I can't.

"It's okay," she says, licking her fingers one by one, the way I always loved. "Admit it. Doesn't it give you the most thrilling fever?"

"Yes," I say, putting my purse down on the table and taking an inventory of my pulse, insistent at my navel, the beads of perspiration on my upper lip. "Yes. It does."

And then I remember those nights long ago, the two of us whispering beneath the covers, spinning dreams as light and pink as cotton candy. I remember running hand in hand between the rows of corn, the wind whipping our braids behind us, running till our unsteady legs would no longer hold us up and we collapsed breathless in each other's arms. I remember this and more. And in that moment I gather Molly, warm and solid, in my arms, breathe in the sticky, apple-cherry smell of her, and we laugh.

A CKNOWLEDGMENTS

My niece Elizabeth has reminded me that a young girl is a creature at once radiant and vulnerable. My hopes and fears for her
are in this book.

In writing this novel, I am grateful to more people than I can
possibly list. I would like to acknowledge, first, my agent, Jennie
Dunham, who has been not only a passionate and conscientious
advocate but also a true friend. My editor, Kristin Kiser, provided me with wise and thoughtful insights and suggestions to
help me shape and strengthen the book. Her enthusiasm for and
belief in the novel sustained me during the course of revision. I
am also thankful to Crown attorney Steve Weissman for his
attention and commitment to my manuscript.

I am grateful for the generosity of my thesis committee at

the University of North Carolina at Wilmington. Lindsay Pentolfe Aegerter, in addition to being a willing listener and attentive reader, also has been a good friend. Philip Gerard's candid yet encouraging critiques of my work have helped me grow as both a writer and a reader of fiction. Finally, I want to thank my chair, Rebecca Lee, who has helped me appreciate how fiction allows both writers and readers to appreciate the complexity of human nature and interpersonal relations.

I am likewise grateful to two members of the creative writing faculty at George Mason University, Fairfax, Virginia. Stephen Goodwin, my first fiction instructor, was kind enough to see merit in my early, awkward attempts and to remind me of the importance, first and foremost, of story. He also introduced me to the work of Jean Rhys, whose *Wide Sargasso Sea*, in its portrayal of the madwoman in the attic in *Jane Eyre*, provided inspiration for this book. It is thanks to Susan Shreve that I first read Vladimir Nabokov's *Lolita*. Because of her encouragement, I found the courage to undertake writing such an ambitious first novel.

I would like to thank several other professors at UNCW, first among them, Brooks Dodson. Under his instruction, I completed and published an annotated bibliography of scholarship and criticism on *Lolita* in the *Bulletin of Bibliography*. I could not have written my own novel had I not undertaken such extensive research.

Mike Wentworth shared his books on films and film stars, as well as personal copies of many movies from the 1940s.

In addition, many of the faculty and staff at UNCW have been valued mentors and friends, among them Paula Kamenish, Sue and Steph Richardson, Ele Byington, Pat Coughlin, Deb Gay, Kelly Easton, Dan Noland, Barbara Waxman, and Don Bushman. Michael White has generously read my short fiction and provided valuable critiques. He and Kathleen Halme of Western Washington University helped hone my sense of imagery and language.

Three friends gave me opportunities to work and school their horses while I wrote the novel, providing me with a therapeutic counterpoint to my long hours at the computer. They are Barbara Long, Sandra Melton, and Robb Prichard and their horses Commander, Scarlett, and Andy.

I want to recognize my students, whose grace and energy have inspired me throughout my graduate teaching career.

I am blessed with many friends, whose gifts of laughter, late-night talks, good food, and perspective have been a source of tremendous strength. While I will certainly overlook some whose names should appear here, in addition to those already mentioned, I would like to thank especially Stacey McCann, Wendi Kaufman, Dawn Radford, Kaitlyn Allocco, Marijke Philipsen, Lauri Rice, Annette DiLascio, Marguerite Duffy, Gordon Binder, Christy Fisher, Monica Ferrare, Paul Gallagher, Frank Tascone, John Ware, Lucille Lisle, Jan Meads, Jamie Trost, Angie Ackerman, Suzanne and Beth Yenchko, Judy Marsilio Whitaker, Tonda Rush, Mark Sheehan, Betty Sullivan, Roz Stark, Steve Emslie, Meryl Learnihan, Tilia Klebenov, Vince Moore,

Bill DiNome and Deborah Flora, Mary Sherwood, Anne Dykers, Alesia Montana, Dee Casey, Stuart Kaplan, Page Paterson, Michelle Manning, Michelle Frazier, and Michelle Burchard-Lewis. Michael Dean has provided not only lifelong friendship but also freelance work that has kept me afloat during the lean years.

My dog Hoppy has been a constant companion on walks and at the computer throughout more than fifteen years. He has made the solitary life of a writer less lonely.

My brother Martin Jones, professor of mathematics at the College of Charleston, South Carolina, and my second cousin Janet Lambert, former professor of reading and literacy at Eastern Illinois University, Charleston, Illinois, encouraged me to take the plunge and return to school at age forty to pursue a career in fiction writing and teaching. My brother Bradley Jones and his wife, Robin, have likewise been enthusiastic about my decision. The energy and antics of my niece Alexandra and nephew Adam also sustain me and make me laugh.

I have also found strength in the examples of my grandmothers, Irene Quivey and Hazel Jones; my aunt, Joan Quivey; and my great-aunt, the late Mabel McCracken. My uncle, Robert Quivey, has extended himself to me in important ways on more than one occasion, and my cousins Rob, David, Barb, and Eric and their spouses and children have expanded my sense of family.

My father, Clifford Jones, has provided not only financial assistance, but more important, a recognition of the value and joy in self-discipline and hard work. I needed both in abundance to finish this project.

Finally, I am grateful to my mother, Jean Quivey Jones, who died March 12, 1998, of complications from a childhood bout with rheumatic fever. When I was still quite young, Mom instilled in me a love of reading and writing that continues to this day. I would not be the woman I am now had it not been for her. In November 1997, when she was hospitalized with pneumonia, I called her on the phone every morning, and she told me stories of growing up in the 1940s, many of which have made their way in some form into this book. A line from her journal also appears in the novel. I will never forget her, nor the legacy she left me.